THE COMPLETELY USELESS ENCYCLOPEDIA

THE COMPLETELY USELESS ENCYCLOPEDIA

(INCORPORATING THE JUNIOR *DOCTOR WHO* BOOK OF LISTS)

Chris Howarth and Steve Lyons

First published in Great Britain in 1996 by
Doctor Who Books
an imprint of Virgin Publishing Ltd
332 Ladbroke Grove
London W10 5AH

ISBN 0 426 20485 9

Typeset by Galleon Typesetting, Ipswich
Printed and bound in Great Britain by
Mackays of Chatham PLC

CONTENTS

In Memory of Godzilla
1954–95

ABOUT THIS BOOK

Following the huge success of our *Red Dwarf Programme Guide* (£4.99 from all good booksellers), Virgin thought they'd be on to a nice little earner if they commissioned a spate of similar volumes, devoted to such cult-telefantasy classics as *EastEnders* and *Neighbours*. When most of these books actually reached the shops without being shredded, we thought 'Yeah, we'll 'ave a bit o' that'. Despite the fact that neither of us is gay, we elected to submit a proposal for a volume covering *The Tomorrow People*, it being ITV's longest-running SF series. Alas, it transpired that nobody outside the Editorial Department at Virgin had heard of either version. Nor were they keen to let us write about *Prisoner: Cell Block H* or the *Mighty Morphin' Power Rangers*.

There was nothing else for it: despite the fact that neither of us is gay, we had to submit an outline for a *Doctor Who* book! Not that we're suggesting Virgin will publish any old crap with the programme's name on it (Boxtree's output would seem to disprove this), but at least we could be fairly sure they'd heard of it. The question was, what aspect of *Who* could we cover that: a) hadn't been done to death; and b) would require minimal research, or none whatsoever? The answer was surprisingly simple: we'd compile a complete alphabetical guide to everything we could remember off-hand about the series. Needless to say, the proposal was duly accepted.

We have tried to avoid dull things like technical details and plot synopses, and to concentrate on what makes being a *Doctor Who* fan so enjoyable. This includes collecting duff items of merchandise for no reason, nitpicking each story, seeking out amusing misprints in other people's work (so, hopefully, our proof-readers will be very careful not to make us look stupid) and, of course, taking the piss out of other fans. Naturally, there's nothing personal meant by this, so if we do happen to slag off your book, script, piece of artwork or acting ability, please don't be offended, it's only because we love you really. Apologies too to people outside the UK who don't understand the parochial references to British TV programmes and personalities. We were asked not to include these, but if we'd taken out everything that Virgin weren't sure about (obscenities, libellous phrases, etc), the book would have been about ten pages long.

A number of good ideas have, sadly, fallen by the wayside. We did want to hire a superb artist to provide some lavish illustrations, but we were told that we could only spend a fiver. We decided to take the cash and do the job ourselves, and we think we've completed it to a professional standard. *Nope, the pictures were too awful even for Virgin. So I kept the fiver – Ed.* Virgin also declined to publish eight versions of the book, each with a different cover. We had suggested this in the best interests of fans – who would be able to buy a copy featuring their favourite Doctor – and not as a blatant attempt to rip them off. We've ended up with a homage to that seminal item of merchandise, the TARDIS tin, which housed the 'Trial of a Time Lord' videos. This briefly inspired us to write lots more than we had intended, in the hope of making the book thick enough to double as an attractive TARDIS model. But we couldn't be bothered.

We should thank all those people who've reminded us of interesting things about *Doctor Who*, or who've just made up jokes that we've stolen. However, a full list would take up several pages and we'd probably insult lots of friends by forgetting them, so let's just say that this book is dedicated to fans everywhere. And no, you're not all getting a free copy.

We hope you enjoy reading *The Completely Useless Encyclopedia*, but since we've got your money by now, we can't really pretend to be all that bothered.

Chris Howarth and Steve Lyons,
The Planet Dildo, 1996

THE OBLIGATORY *DOCTOR WHO* EPISODE GUIDE

FIRST DOCTOR (WILLIAM HARTNELL)

Season One

A ~~100,000 BC~~ ~~The Tribe of Gum~~ An Unearthly Child
B ~~The Mutants~~ ~~The Dead Planet~~ The Daleks
C ~~Beyond the Sun~~ ~~Inside the Spaceship~~ The Edge of Destruction
D ~~Journey to Cathay~~ Marco Polo
Oh, sod this for a game of soldiers . . .

A

'AAH!': Uncharacteristic exclamation uttered by a Cyberman, to itself, upon discovering 'the ones from the TARDIS' in 'The Five Doctors'. Sadly, this immortal comment was omitted from the re-edited special edition video. This may have made the scene more realistic, but it certainly detracted from its entertainment value. Still, we did get back the priceless moment in which the fifth Doctor's lascivious gaze makes plain his feelings for Susan. A fair trade-off, then.

A DAY WITH A TV PRODUCER: Book describing a surprisingly hectic day in the life of John Nathan-Turner. Such was John's dedication that he even found time in his busy schedule to approve some merchandise that had come out several years previously. *A Day with a TV Producer* was noteworthy because it featured Peter Davison's first appearance in a *Doctor Who* publication, over a year before he was cast in the role. Yeah, so maybe he was only on a tiny photo pinned to JN-T's wall, but it counts.

AGGEDOR: Ferocious creature that lived in the caverns beneath the Citadel of Peladon and which came to be revered as a sacred animal by the locals. The writer of the 'Curse of Peladon' video cover-copy mistook it for an Agador: an altogether more placid

3

beast that enjoys pushing pineapples and grinding coffee.

ARIDIUS: World on which the Doctor, Ian, Barbara and Vicki were captured by ferocious Muppets, but managed to escape when a gigantic testicle flopped through the wall of their prison. Dodgy effects weren't the Aridians' only problem, however. They tempted fate unwisely when naming their nice, comfortable planet, for, sure enough, it soon became arid. A similar mistake was made by the people who sent an advance force of Mechanoids to a world that they christened Mechanus, expecting them not to take it over.

'ARMAGEDDON FACTOR, THE': Okay then, BBC Video, tell us this: if you could manage to squeeze six episodes of this story on to a single video tape, why did you find it impossible to do likewise with 'The Sea Devils', 'Planet of the Spiders', 'The Seeds of Doom', etc? Bet you didn't even try.

ASBESTOS: Harmful substance discovered at BBC Television Centre in 1988. The *Doctor Who* team were forced to leave the building and film 'The Greatest Show in the Galaxy' in a tent, resulting in a more suspenseful and realistic production than had been intended.

'ASTOUNDING STORIES OF THE OUTER SPACE ROBOT PEOPLE OF TELEVISION'S *DR WHO*': What you'd be able to read if you owned a copy of *The Dalek Book*, an annual-format publication from 1964. Although their covers lacked similar boasts, it's logical to assume that equally astounding stories could be found within the pages of the two follow-ups, *The Dalek World* and *The Dalek Outer Space Book*.

The Dalek World does however reveal some interesting, if a little hard to swallow, facts about the creatures from Skaro. They weigh only two pounds and can travel at 2000 miles-per-hour along the M1, enabling them to cover the distance between Birmingham and London in around two minutes. (Oh yeah. What about the 70 miles-per-hour speed limit?) When they arrived in London they'd then be able to power the entire city from the electrical energy they generate – if they felt like it, that is. One of their weaknesses is a failure to see the colour red, which, judging by the accompanying illustration, means that they are forever smashing into post boxes, probably at 2000 miles-per-hour. If they can't see that particular colour what were those red movie Daleks doing, though? We suppose they must have been a diabolical attempt to create some invisible spies, which the Daleks mistakenly believed had worked perfectly. The least believable claim in the feature is that the Abominable Snowmen of the Himalayas are actually Dalek survivors of a crashed spaceship who crawled out of their casings. Unbelievable, not because it contradicts the series but because it's bloody daft: who'd mistake a little green-tentacled blob for a huge great hairy thing?

The third in the series, *The Dalek Outer Space Book*, was the last, presumably because the publishers had completely run out of astounding stories and interesting Dalek facts. Actually, they couldn't quite come up with enough of either to fill this book, hence a none-too-exciting adventure for Chris Welkin – Planeteer.

ATMOSPHERIC DENSITY JACKETS: Space anoraks.

5

B

BAG, THE DOCTOR'S: Handy plot device introduced into the *TV Comic* strip by artist Bill Mevin (currently doing sterling work on 'The Perishers', by the way). Remember how when Felix the Cat got into a fix he'd reach into his bag of tricks? Well, that's pretty much what Dr Who did with this seemingly dimensionally transcendental case. For example, if he, John and Gillian needed to do some swimming to escape the clutches of a fearsome land-based creature, he'd pull out three pairs of flippers. There was another occasion when Father Christmas needed some extra toy TARDISes to meet demand from children, and Dr Who rummaged around and produced a toy-replicator. No, honestly, it's true.

'BALLAD OF THE LAST CHANCE SALOON': The addition of a sing-along-a-Lynda-Baron version of the plot to 'The Gunfighters' made a novel change from the usual stock music; just as the plot itself was a refreshing break from those historicals in which the whole thing was taken seriously and the correct people died at the end. This was, however, a missed opportunity for the record industry. Even now, it's not too late. They could get Lynda, and Peter Purves, into the recording studio to lay down a fantastic new mix (and Jackie Lane, too; her piano playing was magnificent for somebody who had never tried it before). The B side, of course, would be 'Business is Business' by Judith Hibbert, that rock classic from *The Ultimate Adventure*.

BANDRELL AMBASSADOR: See MONSTERS THAT LOOK A LOT LIKE SOCKS WITH HANDS STUCK UP THEM.

BARABARA: Leech-like monsters that featured in the early Marvel comic strip 'City of the Damned' (or 'City of the Cursed', if you read the inexplicably censored American reprint). Not to be confused with Barbara, who was a respected companion of the first Doctor and not monstrous at all, unless you count her hairdo.

BARBARAVILLE: One of several places in the UK that were surely named after the first Doctor's schoolteacher companions. Others include Ianstown, Wright's Green and several Chestertons. See also the accompanying list.

<hr>

TEN BRITISH PLACE NAMES THAT COULD HAVE BEEN CHOSEN BY *DOCTOR WHO* FANS

1: Padbury.
2: Bernice. A contender for the spiritual home of New Adventures readers (Cartmel is another).
3: Elishaw. Short for Elizabeth Shaw, no doubt, and thus named by either a *Doctor Who* fan or a chocolate fetishist.
4: East and West Perry. The name might be spelt wrong, but the geography is spot on.
5: Great Sutton. There are two of these, presumably in homage to both Sid and Sarah; alternatively, Sutton Courtenay combines them both with the actor who played the Brigadier, at least according to BBC Audio.
6: Drax. Unfortunately this is nowhere near Brixton.

7: Gell. Presumably this village is full of guards. No? Oh well, please yourselves.
8: World's End. A popular episode; no less than five conurbations have taken its name. That's five more than have called themselves 'The Death of Doctor Who', for a start.
9: Kemble. If the village is anything like the planet, steer clear. A few miles east and you could visit Sarn instead.
10: Hanging Langford.

BARNES COMMON: London location where Ian Chesterton, returning from an unsuccessful job interview as an assistant research scientist at a Reigate rocket components firm, first encountered Susan and an unconscious Barbara following a car accident. Oh yes he did. It said so in the book *Doctor Who in an Exciting Adventure with the Daleks*, and still said as much when it was reprinted by Target as *Doctor Who and the Daleks*. One possible explanation for this deviation from accepted facts is that Ian, as the book's narrator, embellished things a little. He probably thought that being a rocket scientist was a sight more glamorous than teaching at Coal Hill School. But if that's the case, why didn't he just claim to have got the job of chief research scientist, or president of the company? It's no surprise that Ian thought his encounter with the so-called Tribe of Gum too dull to recount, but why did Target later feel the need to pretend that Jo Grant's debut story was *Doctor Who and the Doomsday Weapon*?

BASSETT, BERTIE: Composite creature with liquorice allsorts for body parts, which serves as the edible mascot of confectionery firm Bassetts. Its copyright owners were a bit miffed when 'The Happiness Patrol' featured a completely dissimilar composite creature

9

with liquorice allsorts for body parts. *Doctor Who*'s Kandyman was perhaps more difficult to take seriously than, say, the big-screen villain of the same name. Nevertheless, it committed some extremely naughty acts, which, we are legally bound to point out, have never been mimicked by Bertie Bassett nor by any sweets whose primary ingredient is the root of the glycyrrhiza glabra plant.

BATMAN: One of the world's first costumed heroes, Batman was created by Bob Kane and premiered in *Detective Comics* issue 27 in 1939, graduating to his own title in 1940. The nocturnal career of millionaire Bruce Wayne brought him into contact with such colourful and enduring villains as the Joker, the Penguin, the Riddler and Catwoman. Many of these were given a new lease of life by the fondly remembered sixties TV series starring Adam West, with Burt Ward as kid sidekick Robin (alias Wayne's ward Dick Grayson). The comic-books introduced Commissioner Gordon's daughter Barbara as a second Batgirl (the first was tennis ace Betty Kane) so that she could spin off into the show. Michael Keaton and Val Kilmer have more recently portrayed Batman on the big screen (the latter in the ironically titled *Batman Forever*), with George Clooney set to take over. An animated series in a similar style has also proved successful. Batman now stars in four monthly comic-books, and latter-day writers have emphasised the 'Dark Knight' aspect of his persona with storylines such as the Joker's murder of the second Robin, Jason Todd, and the breaking of Batman in the classic *Knightfall* series. He is mentioned in 'Inferno' and 'The Time Monster'.

BATMOBILE: And a model of this was seen in 'The Talons of Weng-Chiang'.

BBC ARCHIVES: Contained within these hallowed vaults, preserved for posterity by a far-sighted corporation, are the all-time classics of British television, including several episodes of *Doctor Who*, and even a few with Patrick Troughton.

BBC 3: Fanciful notion that rather damaged the plausibility of 'The Dæmons'. Asking an audience to accept animated gargoyles and huge demonic aliens is fair enough, but the idea of the Beeb being able to fund a further terrestrial channel, now that is stretching things.

BBC VIDEO: Hey, what a fantastic idea: suspend the *Doctor Who* releases to avoid confusing people while the American TV version is current. That's brilliant! Without a monthly video to buy, fans are bound to completely forget that there were seven other Doctors before Paul McGann. Would we appear a little cynical if we suggested the decision may have been sales motivated? If so, it wasn't too clever to hack out the action scenes (we can't have twelve-year-olds finding out that guns hurt people – it might put them off using them), delay release by a week, and charge fifteen quid for the thing, was it?

BEATLES, THE: Popular beat combo from the sixties, whose 'Ticket to Ride' was considered to be classical music by Vicki and an excuse to hand-jive by Ian. Their mop-top hairstyles came back into fashion during the 57th segment of time, and were all the rage amongst the Monoid community. The Movellans tried to follow suit, but were hampered by their too-literal robot brains: their attempts to become hip consisted of wearing stringy mop heads and almost outdoing Ian in the dancing stakes when attacked.

11

BEDROOM SCENES: Sleeping arrangements within the TARDIS have been the subject of much speculation. An early attempt was made to scotch the more salacious rumours by showing that the crew rested, fully clothed, on reclined pallets. In the permissive eighties, however, a more liberal attitude was taken. During Peter Davison's tenure it seemed that hardly a week could pass without the cameras intruding upon his companions' nocturnal arrangements. Only Turlough and the Doctor himself escaped such prying. We watched as Nyssa built an enormous vibrator in her bedroom and as Tegan was entered by a giant snake in hers. But the final insult came in 'The King's Demons', as the Doctor described a king-sized bed to Tegan as 'Another way of keeping warm'. By *Doctor Who*'s formerly pristine standards, this was practically the equivalent of full-frontal sex, and we were shocked.

'BEDWETTING FOR BEGINNERS': Advertising feature that took half a page in the thirtieth anniversary issue of *Doctor Who Magazine* (issue 207), despite the best efforts of editor Gary Russell. Someone at ERIC – the Enuresis Resource and Information Centre – must have thought this a good way of reaching sufferers. Readers were encouraged to ferret out potential incontinents amongst their classmates or social groups of ten-year-olds. To assist them, lots of information about 'wee or urine as the doctor calls it' was presented, alongside some disturbingly graphic diagrams. It would be interesting to know how many people responded to the ad; not many, we suspect, although excitement over 'Dimensions in Time' may have caused a spike in the figures.

BEHIND THE SOFA: Location to which younger viewers traditionally fled at the sight of *Doctor Who* monsters. We consider it extremely dangerous to thus encourage the belief that household furniture can protect against lethal discharges of energy and suchlike. A fast-acting remedy for such behaviour – or, alternatively, an amusing prank for irresponsible parents – would be to secrete a full-sized Dalek behind your couch.

BENNETT: The single suspect in the not-so-complex murder mystery that was 'The Rescue'. Unsurprisingly, he dunnit, although for some reason he had to dress up and call himself Koquillion first. Many years later, an image of Koquillion appeared to the third Doctor at the behest of the Keller machine, as one of his greatest fears. As the costume itself is unterrifying, this was perhaps symbolic of the Doctor's worry that he might overlook such an obvious resolution again.

BENNY: Lumbering, simple-minded farmhand from *Crossroads*. Those who remember the character will know that he automatically springs to mind every time the other Benny is mentioned in the New Adventures. Most annoying, that.

BERNARD: Thinly veiled reference to British Rocket Group scientist Professor Bernard Quatermass in 'Remembrance of the Daleks'. Scriptwriter Ben Aaronovitch was no doubt aware of Nigel Kneale's low opinion of *Doctor Who*, hence his reluctance to blatantly mention the name 'Quatermass' and perhaps risk having the good professor's creator go ballistic.

BESSIE: The Doctor's yellow roadster, etc, etc. One of the most disappointing aspects of growing up during the Pertwee era was the surprising lack of a die-cast toy version from either Dinky or Corgi. We didn't want much; it didn't have to come in a gift set with a UNIT jeep and assorted plastic monsters (although that would have been nice); even a small Matchbox one would have sufficed. Sadly, the nearest anyone came to producing it was a model of 'Gabriel', the yellow vintage car driven by Father Unwin in Gerry Anderson's *The Secret Service*. But that was just flipping typical – Gerry-flaming-Anderson fans got the lot! It's as if they sat there at Dinky HQ going 'Oh look, that minor character in *Joe 90* is driving a car, let's mass produce it' and 'That Gerry Anderson's got an idea for a new programme called *The Investigator*. It probably won't ever become a series, but why don't we make some toy cars based on it anyway?' It came as no comfort to learn recently that a couple of firms had indeed expressed an interest in licensing a toy Bessie. Though that kind of thing happens quite a lot, you know . . .

TEN PLANNED ITEMS OF *DOCTOR WHO* MERCHANDISE THAT DIDN'T REACH THE SHOPS

1: The Whomobile by Corgi Toys. By the time they'd got the prototype ready, the vehicle had disappeared from the programme.

2: Daleks by Corgi Toys. Two different versions, actually: one was good, so it's a pity it didn't see the light of day; the other was crap, so it's just as well it didn't.

3: *Doctor Who Discovers Miners*. Along with *Doctor Who Discovers Inventors* and *Doctor Who Discovers Pirates*, this was another proposed book in the educational Target series. Oh, what a shame, it sounds *sooo* exciting. What next, we wonder: *Doctor Who Discovers Car Park Attendants*?

4: The Whomobile by Dapol. Probably due to coincide with the release of their third Doctor figure, which didn't come out either. What with the proposed range of twelve-inch figures and everything, we could practically have based this entire list on Dapol prototypes.

5: 'Jamie's Awae in his Time Machine'. This would have been the follow-up to Frazer Hines's 'Who is Doctor Who', had that record done anything. We're lost for words, unlike Frazer apparently.

6: *Doctor Who Weekly* issue 44, although they had the cover ready and everything. And speaking of comics . . .

7: *Marco Polo* – the Comic Strip. Plans to adapt this Hartnell historical into strip form were thwarted by *TV Comic*'s exclusive rights to do all that kind of thing. Perhaps it's for the best, as they'd be rare collectors items by now and those soddin' dealers would be charging a fortune.

8: K9 Bubble Bath. Intended as a companion to the Dalek Bubble Bath – a vaguely Dalek-shaped item produced by a company called, appropriately enough, The Water Margin. A clever name wasn't enough to keep the company afloat, however; they got out of their depth and the K9 idea was torpedoed.

9: Susan and Sarah Jane 'Five Doctors' postcards. Actually, these were both available during the autograph sessions at the Longleat Celebration, but they weren't very flattering, and after the event quantities of them could be found dumped in the bushes.

10: *Christmas on a Rational Planet* with the lurid yellow cover and the artwork that made Sylvester McCoy look like Jasper Carrott. Blimey, imagine that, a New Adventures cover rejected because it's not up to standard.

'BEYOND THE SUN': Everyone seems to agree that this was the title of an early *Doctor Who* story, but no one can decide which one.

BILLY: Young Welshman who went with the Chimeron Queen Delta to help repopulate her planet. Nice work if you can get it.

BLACK GUARDIAN: An evil bloke with a talent for disguise. He fooled the Doctor into thinking he was his own good counterpart by cunningly swapping his black robes for white, whilst a more ambitious headmaster costume earnt him access to the beds of many a public schoolboy. His headdress was also useful for those occasions when you just have to hide in a pond and pretend to be a duck, although sadly we never saw this ruse in action.

BLACKLIGHT, THE ART OF ANDREW SKILLETER: Yeah, just what the world needs, an expensively packaged collection of artwork from book covers, video sleeves, etc, which anyone who's in the least bit interested will doubtless already have on the original book covers, video sleeves, etc.

BLACKPOOL: Northern seaside town that was on the tip of the Doctor's tongue in 'Revelation of the Daleks'. Good thing he didn't get there, as he would have walked into a trap set by the Celestial Toymaker. In real life, Blackpool was the site, for many years, of the DWAS's annual orgy (sorry, we mean 'conference'); hardly surprising, as it hosted the biggest *Doctor Who* Exhibition of the time. A wonderful TARDIS shell beckoned tourists into its over-sized innards, within which you could thrill to real costumes and props and, better still, spend hours playing with the controls in a mock-up console room, though most of them did naff all. The Exhibition also contained a shop, which was the best place ever for merchandise. Its plethora of unique stickers, pencils, rubbers, cups, etc, would have filled any sad completist's shelves. Nor did the excitement end there! At the Pleasure Beach down the road, a sign proclaimed that an exciting adventure with Doctor Who was to be had in one of the attraction's arcades.

Alas, it was a downright lie, but an exploration of other sea-front outlets would always yield rewards, whether a moving TARDIS ride (it went up and down, not forwards and backwards through time) or a Dalek on an indoor roundabout. For a few years there was even a collection of *Doctor Who* monsters amongst the resort's famous illuminations. Nowadays, Blackpool's appeal has dramatically faded. The TARDIS has been turned back into a boring old porch, which stands as a monument to what fans have lost. The rides have been scrapped, and there is only one small, sad reminder of a glorious heyday: though Colin Baker never got to film on the Pleasure Beach, a plaque confirms that he, in his 'Doctor Who' persona, opened its Space Invader ride in 1984.

BLACK SMARTIE: K9's downfall. Failing to recognise that this sweet was in fact representative of a black hole, he lost 'The Ultimate Challenge' and was hurled into the sun by a cruel and vengeful seventh Doctor. This cosmic gameshow, in which the mechanical mutt competed with latterday companion Ace and alien dork Cedric, formed the basis of an episode of the BBC's *Search Out Science* series. Its remit was to educate children about the nature of space, although its implication that you can zip around it on a hoverpad, breathing and talking, could be seen as a bit of a bum steer. When the 'Search Out Space' episode aired in 1991, fans prayed that it wouldn't be remembered as an ignominious final outing for *Doctor Who*. Two years later, they learnt a painful lesson about being careful what you wish for.

BLAND, ROBIN: Pseudonym adopted by Terrance Dicks for 'The Brain of Morbius', as he felt that interference with his script had indeed rendered it bland.

This, we think, is a brilliant idea, the potential for which has yet to be exploited. Imagine: 'That's my favourite line – if you take it out, I'm blummin' well changing my name to Timothy Drivel.' Or: 'I'd like to be credited as Bert Thescripteditorisatosser, please.'

BLINOVITCH LIMITATION EFFECT: Regulatory law of time travel, restricting the convergence of an individual and his past or future counterparts. Transgression will result in devastating consequences – unless it's the Doctor having one of his anniversary get-togethers.

BLUE PETER: Long-running live 'magazine' programme for kids, which included features on *Doctor Who* from time to time. Sadly, these were usually the same feature with different voice-overs. We do have them to thank, though, for the availability of the first Doctor's regeneration scene, but if they hadn't borrowed the episode in the first place we might have the whole thing. An appearance by Richard Hurndall and Peter Davison is also notable, as is a demonstration of the Whomobile by Jon Pertwee to then-presenter Peter Purves, and the accidental use of the phrase 'What a beautiful pair of knockers!' by Simon Groom, in reference to a couple of door adornments (nothing to do with *Doctor Who*, but worth watching). Best of all, *Blue Peter* was invaluable for those of us who wanted to make replicas of monsters and associated paraphernalia from egg boxes and sticky-backed plastic. Their DIY triumphs included a *Doctor Who* puppet theatre (the same one that they'd told us how to make for many other characters), for which fantastic cut-out figures of the Doctor and Leela were included in that week's *Radio Times*. And then there was the famous Design-a-Monster competition, won by a Steel

Octopus, a Hypnotron and an Aquaman. The BBC Visual Effects Department built the things, and a damn sight more convincing than some of the Doctor's 'real' foes they were too. Indeed, before this particular clip was unearthed from the archives, fan lore had it that the winning monsters had been the Krotons, the prize being inclusion in an actual story. Nowadays, we have to find another excuse for them. For the sake of completeness, we should mention that Ace often wore a much-coveted *Blue Peter* badge – in real life the property of Sophie Aldred. All this and presenting stints by Janet Ellis ('The Horns of Nimon'), Sarah Greene ('Attack of the Cybermen') and the afore-mentioned Peter Purves. (Flippin' 'eck, they've even got a presenter called Romana now!) Anyone who considers themselves a *Doctor Who* completist should really feel obliged to collect the entire run of this programme too.

BOGDANOFF, IGOR ET GRICHKA: Dark-haired brothers whose images, for reasons best known to the French, adorned both front and back covers of their translations of Target's *Docteur Who* books.

TEN *DOCTOR WHO* NOVELISATIONS FROM OTHER LANDS

1: *Le docteur Who entre en scène* (*Doctor Who and an Unearthly Child*, France). Well, if they had to change the title at least they didn't plump for '100,000 BC'.
2: *Doctor Who en het dodelijke wapen* (*Doctor Who and the Doomsday Weapon*, the Netherlands).
3: *Dr Who – Kampf um die Erde* (*Doctor Who and the Dalek Invasion of Earth*, Germany). Blimey, who translated this one? Adolf Hitler?
4: *Doctor Who und das Komplott der Daleks* (*Doctor Who*

and the Dalek Invasion of Earth, Germany again).
Dunno what a komplott is, but it can't be German for
invasion . . .

5: *Doctor Who und die Invasion der Daleks* (Ha, fooled
you this time: this one's actually the German edition of
Doctor Who and the Daleks).

6: *Doutor Who e os Monstros das Cavernas* (*Doctor Who
and the Cave-Monsters*, Portugal).

7: *Doutor Who e os Demonios Marinhos* (*Doctor Who and
the Sea Devils*, Portugal).

8: *Doutor Who e os Daleks* (Bet you think this is the
Portuguese version of *Doctor Who and the Daleks*,
don't you? Well you're right, it is).

9: *Docteur Who – Meglos* (A tough one this, so after
hours of poring over a French/English dictionary with
no luck at all, we decided to go for a wild stab at: *Doctor
Who – Meglos*).

10: *Doctor Who and the Revenge of the Cybermen* (*Doctor
Who and the Revenge of the Cybermen*, USA).

(There were some Turkish books that looked a bit promising too, but they turned out to be about some bloke by the
name of Doctor Kim, whoever he is. And don't think for one
moment that we considered trying to translate any of the
Japanese titles.)

BONDED POLYCARBIDE ARMOUR: What a load
of old tosh. Everyone knows that Dalek outer casings
are constructed from Dalekenium; hence the well-
known phrase 'Whenever a spectro-scanner registers
Dalekenium you know there are Daleks around'. The
Emperor Dalek's casing is of course made from the
blue-veined gold metal mined on the Skarosian moon
Flidor, which is fused with quartz and the sap of the
arkellis flower. See **J** for more of this kind of stuff.

BOND, JAMES BOND: *Doctor Who* fans are forever
harping on about the supposedly uncanny coincidences

of parallel development between their favourite TV series and the 007 movies. What they all neglect to mention is the fact that the Bond films are huge-budgeted extravaganzas, which have been seen by a large percentage of the world's population. No parallels to be drawn there, then.

BRIDGE STREET, THE TRAIN OVER: As viewers of the London-based soap *EastEnders* know, trains can only run over Walford's Bridge Street with the aid of visual effects. It was quite an honour, then, for 'Dimensions in Time' to be able to show such a vehicle for just the second time in eight years. Unfortunately, it says something about *Doctor Who*'s budget that the earlier attempt was more realistic. See also FOWLER, ARTHUR and RON, BIG.

BRONSON, MISTER: Although he wasn't named, we all know that Susan's headmaster, seen in 'Remembrance of the Daleks', was Mr Bronson from *Grange Hill*. A well-deserved promotion, we think. The question is, how did he get back to 1963?

TEN *GRANGE HILL* STAFF MEMBERS WHO'VE ALSO STARRED IN *DOCTOR WHO*

1: Mr Robson (Stuart Organ) in 'Dragonfire', although he didn't do much.
2: Mr Hicks (Paul Jerricho) as the Castellan in 'Arc of Infinity' and 'The Five Doctors'. The latter gave him the opportunity to say 'No, not the mind probe' before dying. *Grange Hill* gave him the opportunity to get thumped by Bullet Baxter.
3: Mr Hankin (Lee Cornes) in 'Kinda'.
4: Mr Curtis (Neville Barber) in *K9 and Company*.
5: Mr Howard (Michael Osborne) in 'The Horns of Nimon'.

6: Mr Malcolm (Christopher Coll) in 'The Seeds of Death' and 'The Mutants'.

7: Mr Thomson (Timothy Bateson), who excelled as Binro the Heretic in 'The Ribos Operation'.

8: Mr Griffiths (George A Cooper) in 'The Smugglers'.

9: Mr Glover (Vincent Brimble) in 'Warriors of the Deep'. Okay, so he wasn't a real member of staff, but he was Chairman of the Board of Governors. We're sure he's more proud of his four episodes as Tarpok, though.

10: Mr Bronson (Michael Sheard) in just about any story you'd care to mention. He was last seen in 'Remembrance of the Daleks', sprawled across a grave which, to judge by its markings, must have belonged to Perpugilliam Brown.

———◆———

BUBBLING LUMP OF HATE: The contents of a Dalek's casing, as scientifically described in 'Death to the Daleks' and immortalised in verse by 'Doctor in Distress'. Simply add some bonded polycarbide armour and – hey, presto! – one metal meanie.

C

CAKE: Unique slice of merchandise inspired by the *Doctor Who* telemovie, and one that will almost certainly leave collectors with a quandary: to eat or not to eat. There can be little doubt that this fondant-topped sponge, filled with strawberry jam and cream, will perish if left on a shelf alongside the script book, novelisation and video spin-off from the production. Only storage in deep-freeze will preserve examples of this limited edition item for the benefit of future generations. Oh sod it, just scoff the damn thing. That's what it's for.

TEN MERCHANDISING SPIN-OFFS FROM 'THE US TELEMOVIE WITH THE PERTWEE LOGO'

1: The video. Well, that was a bit short, wasn't it?
2: The novelisation. The BBC, we're led to believe, decided to remove all offending references to the New Adventures from Gary Russell's book, although the mention of Cheldon Boniface does rather suggest that the editor wasn't familiar with the ones by Paul Cornell.
3: The script book. Okay for what it is, and the cover's nice. Trouble is, it's got that script in it.
4: The watch. Quite appropriate really. You know, 'about time' and all that.
5: The T-shirts. A must for all Time Lords according to the advert. Good, that leaves us out then. The Doctor too, him being half-human and all.

6: Marvel's *Doctor Who Movie Special*. About four pages worth of text stretched out to thirty-six. Talk about being bigger on the inside. You could also find out the ending to the as-yet-untransmitted movie by flicking through the mag in John Menzies.

7: The *Radio Times* postcards. A set of ten, produced as a limited edition. Why, is there a paper shortage or something?

8: The *Radio Times* sixteen-page souvenir pull-out. Would it be cynical to assume that the cut-out token and slip for the cheapo poster offer was printed in this section rather than in the *Radio Times* proper, just so that fans would rush out and buy another copy to keep in mint condition? Well they needn't have bothered, as the Doc was also on the front cover of the actual magazine, so the fans would have done that anyway.

9: *TV Times*. Not really a spin-off, but *Doctor Who* on the cover of *TV Times*! We never thought we'd see the day. True to form, though, they couldn't resist sticking the ubiquitous soap character on there too; fortunately for fans it was 'Dimensions in Time's' Grant Mitchell. Inside, a fun *Doctor Who* quiz concluded with: 'How many lives does the Doctor have?' Ironic, really, as the entire production team would have got that wrong (see TWELVE).

10: The mouse mat. Eight quid, and you can achieve the same effect as with the back of a Cornflakes box.

CAMELOT: Theme park based at Charnock Richard in Lancashire, which, for some reason or other, the Doctor attempted to save in a future incarnation.

CANCELLATION CRISIS: Label commonly applied to *Doctor Who*'s suspension for a whole eighteen months in 1985/6, which was actually quite distressing at the time. It even made the national news! Several tabloids campaigned to get the series back and a number of minor stars risked career and credibility by singing on the charity disc 'Doctor in Distress'.

Meanwhile, BBC1 controller Michael Grade got visibly sick of being lambasted on TV chat shows, which served him right for appearing on so many. *Doctor Who* was eventually recommissioned and the papers congratulated themselves, not seeming to notice that the suspension had been served in full. It's possible, though, that they prevented the axing of a popular show for which BBC bosses had a personal dislike – at least for a while. But there was yet one more insult to come. A press release confirmed that a reversion to 25-minute slots would give the new season more episodes, but a secret BBC memo, accidentally faxed to the DWAS (yeah, like we believe that!), revealed that 'more episodes' meant fourteen, not twenty-six. Deceptive bastards! One more promise – that the show would be refreshed and improved by its rest – was broken by the replacement of promising (and paid-for) scripts with 'The Trial of a Time Lord'.

CANCER: Terminal disease suffered by the Brigadier in the fiftieth New Adventure. He got over it, else the book could hardly have been called *Happy Endings*; however, the fact that we can look into the future and see such things is disturbing. In this way, the possibility of living 'happily ever after' is denied to all characters in the *Doctor Who* universe (see DODO for more proof). Within seconds of dropping, say, Sarah Jane off in 1976, the Doctor can zip forward seventy years and meet her as a raddled old hag on her death bed. We think most viewers would prefer it if he didn't. What will the fiftieth Missing Adventure (if there is one) be like, we wonder? *Sad Endings*, perhaps, in which the fourth Doctor develops a morbid curiosity about the manner of each of his companions' deaths and decides to attend their funerals. By copyrighting this idea, we hope to ensure that it can't happen (unless we're paid lots of cash). We'd rather see another feel-good tome in which the eternal youthfulness and vigour of our heroes is reaffirmed. How about *Happy Endings 2*: a gathering of old chums, unaged, to celebrate the double wedding of sisters Barbara and Polly Wright to Ian and Ben? There, the idea's on the table if Virgin want to call us.

'CARROT JUICE, CARROT JUICE, CARROT JUICE': Famous last words.

'CAT FLAP': The working title for Rona Munro's Season Twenty-six Cheetah People story. Unfortunately, it was broadcast as 'Survival', which has far less potential for juvenile innuendo.

CELERY: Vegetable worn in the manner of a lapel badge by the fifth Doctor. It transpired that its presence was in order to detect certain gases in the praxis range of the spectrum. As we all suspected, really.

CENTAURI, ALPHA: Apparently, when director Lennie Mayne first saw the costume for this alien ambassador, he declared that it looked like a giant penis and ordered that it be fitted with a cloak. Not surprisingly, then, the character as seen on TV looks like a giant penis in a cloak.

CHAPLETTE, ANNE: Huguenot girl assumed to have survived the Saint Bartholomew's Day Massacre thing because Dodo had a surname quite similar to hers. Nope, sorry, they've lost us with that one.

CHATTERTON: Inconspicuous companion to the first Doctor.

CHRONIC HYSTERESIS: A sort of time loop kind of wotsit or something used by Meglos. But that's irrelevant; we include it merely because it sounds nice and silly. And so does 'recursive occlusion'; no idea what that is, though.

CLASSIC: A *Doctor Who* story that is universally accepted as being perfect in all ways, and is thus eligible to join a select Hall of Fame. Once such a designation has been applied, the work in question cannot be denigrated again. For instance, to point out that 'The Caves of Androzani' is only 'The Power of Kroll' with better effects would be totally unacceptable in polite company, and could lead to a fatwah being issued. As all new *Doctor Who* is, by definition, bound to be crap (see FAN REACTION), it is of course impossible to identify and label a classic for a minimum period of three years after transmission. Also, no official mechanism exists for 'declassifying' a story, hence the stony silence when 'The Tomb of the Cybermen' was recovered and, likewise, when 'The Dæmons' was repeated.

CLIFFHANGERS: The end-of-episode cliffhanger was an essential part of *Doctor Who*, at least until the Americans abolished it. It might well have meant that the story itself ground to a halt whilst the companion dashed off and got herself into bother, but when it was done well it could leave viewers on the edge of their seats or, if you're Mary Whitehouse, phoning their MPs in disgust. Episode endings ranged from sudden and melodramatic appearances of old foes to camera zooms into Colin Baker's face at otherwise unexciting junctures. See the accompanying list for some of the more novel examples.

TEN NOTABLE CLIFFHANGERS

1: 'Genesis of the Daleks' part two concluded with Sarah Jane making her way to freedom up some scaffolding. She slipped, she fell, she found herself in a nail-biting freeze-frame . . . and in part three we learnt that there was a platform underneath her. She picked herself up, and she started climbing again.

2: 'The Tomb of the Cybermen' featured none of the eponymous monsters in its first episode, but it did conclude with a very obviously fake Cyberman-shaped firing-range target springing into view. Stand up Justin Richards who, in *Doctor Who Magazine* issue 150, said: 'At the end of part one it's definitely a Cyberman that walks out . . . but in part two . . . it's a dummy on a trolley . . . that really struck me at the time.' Bet you're hoping nobody re-reads that in the light of the video release, eh Justin? Living proof that the memory does cheat after all (see 'THE MEMORY CHEATS').

3: Perhaps the most celebrated cliffhanger ever came in part one of 'Vengeance on Varos', when the Doctor's seeming death is observed from a television control room and the Governor cues the credits by announcing 'And cut it now!' We like this so much that it had to make the list, even though we couldn't think of any way to make it sound amusing.

4: Conversely, the end of 'The Underwater Menace' part three is very amusing indeed, as it features the world's most unconvincing gunshot and an overexcited Professor Zaroff screaming (come on, all together now) 'Nothing in ze vorld can shtop me now!' So impressive that the cameraman has to take a run-up.

5: 'The Space Museum' part three was entitled 'The Search', and finished appropriately with the discovery of the missing Doctor, albeit not by the viewer. As William Hartnell took a holiday during this episode, it was less a case of finding a dramatic place to finish and more one of taking the action as far as it could go without him.

6: 'Dragonfire' part one boasted what became known as the 'literal cliffhanger', as the Doctor dangled himself over a sheer drop for no apparent reason other than that the end of the episode was near. Writer Ian Briggs did the convention circuit, telling curious attendees that they'd have to wait for his forthcoming novelisation to learn the reasoning behind this sequence. Why not go all the way? You might as well show just the first three parts of a story, then announce that the book will contain the fourth.

7: 'The Dæmons' part three. Well, what a tension-filled adventure! Everyone knew that the Doctor and his friends were in no danger, so the best that could be hoped for was a bit of bother for the Master. Will he be able to get out of this one, or will good triumph?

8: 'The Mark of the Rani' part one. The Doctor is hurtling towards certain death and the audience spend seven days trying to figure out how he might avoid it. Then, in true movie serial style, the next week's recap is re-edited to show that he was safe all the time.

9: The separation of 'The Five Doctors' into four episodes provided such memorable cliffhangers as the Master walking down some stairs and Sarah Jane tripping up and rolling down a gentle incline. Ooh, scary.

10: 'The Deadly Assassin' part three frightened Mary Whitehouse, if nobody else. See WHITEHOUSE, MARY.

CLOAKING DEVICE: Replacement for the TARDIS chameleon circuit in 'The US Telemovie with the Pertwee Logo'. The reason given by executive producer Philip Segal was that an American audience wouldn't have understood what a 'chameleon circuit' was. Perhaps we're being naive, but isn't that where the script comes in? They managed to explain it adequately in 1963, so why's it a problem in 1996? There are more chameleons in America than in Britain, so it can't be that difficult a concept. Besides, a 'cloaking device' is commonly held to cause invisibility, to radar and sometimes to the naked eye. It's a different thing

29

altogether, and we have to take a stand before this goes any further. Next thing we know, the console room will become a 'bridge', the dematerialisation circuit will be a 'warp engine' and the Daleks will be rechristened 'alien robots'. An American audience won't understand why the lead character has no real name, so since 'Doctor McCoy' is no longer relevant, perhaps we should refer to the Doctor henceforth as 'James T Kirk'?

COALMEN, THE: John Smith's backing band, according to that mine of information, *The Encyclopedia of the Worlds of Doctor Who*. Presumably, they replaced the more appropriately and wittily named Common Men, whose music was enjoyed by Susan in 'An Unearthly Child'. He didn't let on at the time, but the Doctor must have been a bit of an aficionado of that band too; well, he did borrow their lead singer's name later on. Lucky he wasn't into Dusty Springfield, really.

COMIC STRIPS IN *RADIO TIMES*: 'Dreadnought', the recent eighth Doctor strip (in which our hero is threatened with transformation into a long-haired, big-nosed Cyberman) isn't the first time the Doctor has appeared in comic form in the weekly listings magazine: legendary artist Frank Bellamy drew the third Doctor in a partial adaptation of 'Colony in Space' part one, though why he bothered to do this is another matter entirely. Before that the first Doctor guest-starred in an episode of *Captain Pugwash*: however, if you're now expecting some tasteless joke about Seaman Staines and Master Bates, you're going to be disappointed.

COMPUTER GAMES: Before sell-thru videos and satellite TV, some fans were in danger of having to find a life beyond the small screen. Fortunately, the microchip revolution solved that problem. Considering *Doctor Who*'s subject matter, the first hi-tech tie-in was a fair time in appearing, but appear it did, with Tom Baker's face gracing the cover of *Computer & Video Games* not long after the man himself graced the Australian adverts for Prime computers, making goo-goo eyes at Lalla Ward. Inside this magazine, Atari owners were delighted to find a BASIC program to type into their machines. Nowadays, of course, things have moved beyond that primitive level, and the wealth of sad knowledge available on the internet means that no technology buff need bother to leave the house again. We thought it would help fill the book, though, if we were to list ten past computer greats. So here they are:

TEN COMPUTER GAMES WITH A PASSING *DOCTOR WHO* CONNECTION, AT LEAST

1: That one in *Computer & Video Games*. It pitted the Doctor against the Master in a pyramid, with the participants picked out in glorious 8x8 resolution. Sadly, like many computer games of its type, it needed several days' debugging to make it playable.

2: *Doctor Who: The First Adventure.* Sporting a picture of Peter Davison on its box, this game mimicked the programme's format to the extent of being split into four 'episodes'. We don't know much more about it, as it could only be played on a BBC Micro, and in those days you needed a second mortgage to afford one.

3: *The Mines of Terror.* A more sophisticated game for the sixth Doctor. Its best feature was its inclusion of a mechanical feline companion, presumably inspired by one of John Nathan-Turner's famous lies about the programme (see RUMOURS and SPLINX).

4: *Warlord.* Dunno much about this either, but it was probably about the Doctor fighting some warlord or other, and was, we expect, really good if you like computer games and that kind of thing.

5: *Brides of Dracula*. An interesting release from Gonzo Games, this takes Drac in pursuit of thirteen virgins through the usual Victorian trappings: graveyard, swamp, forest, castle, village – oh, and secret Dalek laboratory, complete with captive virgin (Victoria, no doubt). Imagine our surprise.

6: *Daleks*. Available in the Public Domain for several formats, this pits one player against an unfeasibly large number of the popular monsters. Fittingly, it's impossible to win; the object of the game is merely to survive as long as possible.

7: *Dalek Attack*. So long as you ignore the fact that the Doctor can't leap tall buildings in a single bound and isn't renowned for disintegrating people with laser guns, this is pretty entertaining. Various Doctors and companions appear, although K9 is sod all use.

8: *Doctor Who and the Daleks*. This self-contained, hand-held electronic game came in that irritating card-backed packaging which can't be opened without ruining it. Purchasers faced a terrible choice, then, between making use of their acquisition and keeping it intact for their collections. We don't know any more about this product.

9: Oh all right, we could only find eight, but there's bound to be two more one day, so you can add them on in biro as they appear . . .

———————◆———————

COOKBOOK, THE DOCTOR WHO: 'Ho, ho,' we thought. 'There's bound to be plenty of mickey-taking mileage in this collection of recipes from *Doctor Who* celebs.' Sadly, only Lynda Baron's 'Wrack of Lamb' and Nerys Hughes's 'Todd in the Hole' seemed worthy of a mention – how author Gary Downie refrained from linking Peri and melons we'll never know, and where was Spotted Alpha Centauri in the desserts section? Never mind, though, the potted biography of Jackie Lane is hilarious. Jocelyn Lane from New York, indeed!

CORNFLAKES: The preferred breakfast of fandom, at least according to a 1996 TV advert. Former DWAS co-ordinator Andrew Beech was flown to New Zealand (as, presumably, no black-walled studios were available in the UK) to sit in front of some costumed lunatics and sprinkle sugar from a silly Dalek-shaped bowl. Sorry, Kellogg's, it'll take more than that to usurp Sugar Smacks and Weetabix in fans' affections. Indeed, *TV Zone* reported that some people had found the stunt 'distasteful'. Can't think why; perhaps they don't like corn-based cereal products?

COSTUMED LUNATICS: Media shorthand for 'devotees of the BBC television science-fantasy programme, *Doctor Who*'. The origins of this phrase lie in the fact that some of the latter are, in fact, costumed lunatics. See also *DOCTOR WHO* FANDOM, PUBLIC IMAGES OF.

COURTROOM DRAMA: If the US telemovie was supposed to have such a big budget, why didn't we get the trial scene that featured in the script book? Come on, even 'The War Games' managed to deliver a simple courtroom set – but then, no British production team ever blew ninety per cent of its budget on the console room, did it? Next time, we suggest keeping back some cash with which to actually tell the story. In the meantime, it might have been a good idea to buy in a few crayons or some chalk and at least give us the courtroom sketches. And, while we're at it, what on earth were those girly, squeaky Dalek voices supposed to be? Dunno what they thought was wrong with the classic version, which even graced the BBC trailer, but whatever it was, getting Pinky and Perky in to do the job was not the answer.

'CRAP': Peter Davison's considered opinion of his entire run on *Doctor Who*, as given on the video *The Doctors – Thirty Years of Time Travel and Beyond*.

CRICKET: Interminably dull sport enjoyed by the fifth Doctor. It was interesting that he suddenly acquired a list of earlier cricketing achievements, despite none of his previous incarnations ever showing the remotest interest in the game (well, apart from a few throwaway remarks from the fourth). Should the eighth Doctor ever display any sporting inclination, it is hoped that his preferences will lean towards a more visually entertaining pastime, such as football or topless darts.

CROMER: Resort to which the Brigadier famously thought he had been taken when, in fact, he was on the far side of a Black Hole. This is apparently hilarious, hence its referencing in just about every semi-official video/piece of fan fiction/New Adventure/fanzine article going. Nowadays, the Brig can hardly open his eyes in the morning without thinking 'Oh my God, I'm in Cromer', which suggests some sort of mental disorder in our opinion. Other oft-quoted Brigadier-isms include 'Chap with wings there, five rounds rapid', 'Liberty Hall' and the one about the eyepatch.

CUNNING DISGUISES OF THE MASTER: Funny how those masks always looked so authentic from a distance, and yet when the Master was down and about to be revealed, they suddenly turned into pathetic lumps of rubber with holes in them – and nobody ever suspected! The prodigious disguise skills of the Doctor's arch-foe even extended to his lowering his height to impersonate a telephone engineer in 'Terror of the Autons' (Yates was certainly fooled, although admittedly he was visibly distracted from studying the intruder's face). Perhaps the Master utilised his regenerative abilities to aid him in such feats; this would answer the ages-old conundrum of how he managed to reach his thirteenth incarnation whilst his supposed contemporary was still on his third. Later on, however, with advanced make-up techniques providing more realistic camouflage, the question was no longer how the Master fooled anybody, but rather why he should bother to try. Can anyone think of a single reason why he should have taken the identity of Kalid in 'Time-Flight', except to give Peter Davison a good laugh when he thought the camera wasn't on him?

CURSE OF THE DALEKS, THE: Erm . . . yes, well, you see we don't actually know anything at all about this mid-sixties stageplay. Oh, except that it had some Daleks in it. Probably. But the debut theatrical spin-off must warrant a mention, however cursory. (Cursory. Get it? Oh, please yourselves.) Naturally, we're keen to rectify this lack of info, so if you happen to have lying around any rare and valuable scripts, programmes, photos, etc from this production, please send them to us c/o Virgin and we'll make sure that the play is given more extensive coverage in any subsequent editions of this book. We can't say fairer than that now, can we?

D

DAAK, ABSLOM: Comic book criminal whose punishment was to become a Dalek Killer with a short life expectancy. He bucked the odds, killed lots of Daleks, and went on to become a veteran of the Marvel strips. He even guest-starred in a New Adventure, although since Virgin aren't allowed to use the Daleks, he didn't exactly live up to his job description. Marvel had already made several attempts to spin a successful concept out of *Doctor Who*: the Freefall Warriors and Doctor Ivan Asimoff got nowhere, and Alan Moore withdrew the copyright to the Special Executive after their acclaimed guest appearances with Captain Britain. That just left Abslom, who was promoted to the hilt for about a week. Best of all the publicity ploys was the recording of a theme tune for a non-existent film about the character. This was distributed free with *Doctor Who Magazine* on a floppy and disappointingly square record. Must get round to listening to that one day. See also DEATH'S HEAD.

DÆMONS: Race of hairy-chested aliens, infinitely powerful but for one fatal weakness – a tendency to be thrown into a state of confusion by petite young blondes. Know the feeling.

DALEK ARMY, THE: A rather select group, the

entrance requirement for which was not, as you might expect, to conquer worlds and exterminate humans in the name of the Emperor, but rather to display a basic knowledge of a certain British telefantasy programme. A company called Broadsystem set up a premium-rate telephone line in 1990 to select suitable candidates. Those who called were greeted by a familiar grating voice, which warned of extermination should they fail the intelligence test. The brave and foolhardy who decided to continue were asked five simple multiple choice *Doctor Who* questions, with the Dalek becoming more excited with each right answer until it seemed that a successful conclusion was an orgasmic experience for it. Broadsystem also ran a telephone role-playing game in which the Doctor and Ace landed on Earth in the midst of a Dalek invasion. Apparently, the complex plot involved the Master, but after trying it once and falling victim to a computer glitch without even meeting a Dalek, spending a fiver into the bargain, we decided we could live without knowing the full story.

'DALEK CUTAWAY': The attempts of certain people to change the names by which we know and cherish our *Doctor Who* stories, just because of a bit of scribbling on some early scripts, has caused a furious and vitriolic debate comparable only to that over the European single currency. We are, for example, now supposed to refer to 'An Unearthly Child' by the title '100,000 BC', so called after the year in which it wasn't set; likewise, 'The Massacre' becomes the far more snappy and dramatic 'The Massacre of St Bartholomew's Eve', named for the day on which it didn't occur. Worst of all, however, is the single-episode story with the on-screen title 'Mission to the Unknown', which was apparently not called that at all, but rather 'Dalek Cutaway'. That said, we can't let the authors of *The Discontinuity Guide* get away with claiming that the correct titles are those which have been 'democratically elected' by fandom. By this logic, BBC Enterprises would have to release videos labelled 'Warriors on the Cheap', 'Waste of Time and the Rani', 'Arse of Inanity', 'That Rubbish with the Twins in it', etc. Meanwhile, the revisionist lobby now claim that 'Dalek Cutaway' didn't have the production code T/A after all, but rather DC. In the hope of sparking some controversy, then, we hereby announce that 'Doctor Who and the Silurians' always had the code DWATS, 'The Invasion of Time' was TIT, and SOD was a very popular code, used three times by different production teams. Oh yes, and an early draft of Anthony Coburn's script for the very first story proves that it was, in fact, called 'Verity, here's that thing about the cavemen you wanted, Love Tony'. See also BEYOND THE SUN and the accompanying list.

TEN STORIES WITH SILLY TITLES

1: 'Doctor Who and the Silurians', for obvious reasons – and we don't mean the fact that the monsters in question didn't come from the Silurian era.

2: 'City of Death'. Okay, so there's a city in it and some death. Not very precise though, is it?

3: 'Dimensions in Time'. Similarly meaningless.

4: 'The Two Doctors'. We can see it's got two Doctors in it, but that's hardly dramatic. What next? 'One Doctor and Two Companions'? 'A Doctor and Some Cybermen'? What was wrong with 'The Androgum Inheritance'?

5: 'The Deadly Assassin'. Like some assassins aren't deadly?

6: 'Planet of the Daleks'. Instead of using this title for a Skaro-based story, they gave it to one that should more accurately have been called 'Planet with Some Daleks on it'. Apart from which, the first-episode cliffhanger –

in which a Dalek is discovered on a planet – is rendered less than shocking.

7: 'Death to the Daleks'. Is this supposed to sound dramatic? 'Can the Daleks survive their encounter with the Doctor . . .?'

8: 'Delta and the Bannermen', because it sounds silly and because the working title, 'Flight of the Chimeron', was great.

9: 'Remembrance of the Daleks'. Now they're just sticking any old word in front of 'of the Daleks' and hoping we won't notice.

10: 'Dalek Cutaway' – but then, that's not the story's real name, is it?

◆

DALEK DIET: Particularly useful 'if you've got a figure like a Dalek'; not so good for the rest of us. This was dreamt up by those inventive people at the *Sun* during their campaign to get Colin Baker to lose some weight. Sadly, the diet consisted not of jelly babies, Dalek lollies and Elizabeth Shaw chocolates, as you might reasonably expect from its name, but rather of the usual health food junk. It worked for Baker, though, who was later pictured clad only in a pair of boxer shorts to demonstrate his new slimline waist. For many fans, this was a welcome alternative to the newspaper's more usual fare.

DALEK MOVIES: Held in nostalgic esteem by many, these two films starring Peter Cushing are now regarded as charming period pieces; in fact they're both utter shite.

DAVIDSON, PETER: Someone that *Doctor Who Monthly* believed had taken over from Tom Baker as the star of the long-running BBC science-fiction series they had covered in detail for sixty issues.

DAVROS, TWO-ARMED: Inaccurate toy produced by Dapol as part of a range including the green K9, the five-sided TARDIS console, the scarfless fourth Doctor, the anorexic Cyberman and the model of Ace that looked like Vera Bennett from *Prisoner: Cell Block H*. In all fairness, some of Dapol's output was much better. Sadly, their very accurate Ice Warrior seems to have been unavailable since the fire that gutted the company's factory in Cheshire. Well, they would be the first to go, wouldn't they?

DAY OF ACTION: That fateful date, 30 November 1990, on which frustrated fans (not us) jammed BBC switchboards with requests to bring back their favourite programme (or *Doctor Who*, in many cases). Faced with such a force of public opinion, the Beeb avoided capitulation by the simple expedient of adjusting the number of calls received (allegedly).

DEATH'S HEAD: Mechanoid bounty-hunter. He was introduced as a giant-sized villain in Marvel's licensed *Transformers* comic, but made an unwelcome guest appearance in the *Doctor Who Magazine* strip 'Crossroads in Time' (issue 135). The Doctor reduced his foe to human proportions with a Tissue Compression Eliminator and sent him (somewhat irresponsibly, we thought) to Earth. Once there, Death's Head starred in the flagship book of Marvel UK's new super-hero line and set about spawning a ridiculous number of spin-off titles. Still believing indiscriminate crossovers to be good, Marvel brought back the Doctor for a return bout in *Death's Head* issue 8, which also featured Dogbolter from earlier *Doctor Who Magazine* adventures. The former sparring partners called a truce and the TARDIS took Death's Head to twentieth-century New York – and Four Freedom's Plaza. The Doctor never got to meet the

Fantastic Four, but a *Doctor Strange* crossover was on the drawing board. Then, thankfully, this whole insanity was ended by the sudden collapse of Marvel UK's output. You see, no matter how hard they tried to convince us otherwise, Death's Head was deeply unpopular. Oh yes, they attempted a similar thing with the Sleeze Brothers, too. Remember them? No, didn't think so.

DEVIL'S HUMP: Located in the vicinity of Devil's End. Well, it would have to be wouldn't it?

DIAMOND LOGO: Ah, for those halcyon days when Saturday evenings promised an exciting trip down a haunting silver tunnel of time, at the end of which was formed the reassuringly steadfast image of the definitive *Doctor Who* symbol. For many years, this quadrilateral beauty was associated in the minds of connoisseurs with quality products from the three essential *Doctor Who* LPs to the Key to Time season. Its integrity was preserved when a timely replacement saddled its successor (the 'neon logo') with the eighties glut of cash-in-quick merchandise. (This logo, incidentally, was designed by an uncredited Chris Achilleos; well, that's what he told us and why should he lie? It's not as if he's short of *Doctor Who* stuff for his portfolio.) For a time, the BBC blocked further use of their rhomboid triumph, even when Target complained that the 1987–9 version (the 'crap logo') was impossible to print without a stupid black band behind it. All products, the Beeb decreed, must bear the current design, and besides there was nothing wrong with it and it was mere coincidence that they never used the thing on their own videos. Faced with continuing pressure, however, the corporation relented and the diamond logo was restored to pre-eminence. Sadly, this meant that it was somewhat devalued, having been appropriated by too many projects unworthy of its endorsement (see accompanying list). At least the Americans didn't get to use it: asked at Manopticon 4 why he had overlooked the most popular of all logos in favour of an earlier version, co-executive producer Philip Segal replied that it was too firmly associated with a particular era of *Doctor Who*. Yeah, like the Pertwee logo isn't?

TEN GOOD WAYS OF CASHING IN ON *DOCTOR WHO*

1: Obtain the rights to a few cheap photos and the diamond logo, plaster them on to an equally cheap product – postcards, phone cards, badges, you know the sort of thing – and sell at a profit.

2: Commission a half-decent comic strip, then publish it four times in increasingly desirable formats.

3: Organise a convention and advertise that lots of great guests will be in attendance, but invite only three. On the day, announce to your attendees that the rest couldn't make it.

4: Spend three seconds devising a great name for a new monster, then make sure you keep the rights in someone else's design. If it's a good one, you can bleed money out of it for a lifetime.

5: Go out and find a few celebrities, point a camera at them, get them to say whatever comes to mind and market the result as an exclusive documentary. The stars' involvement with *Doctor Who* can be minimal, if preferred.

6: Release a one-off piece of merchandise, such as a chess set or a pack of trading cards, then follow it up with one or more essential supplements.

7: Release a succession of edited videos of *Doctor Who* stories, wait until most fans have bought them, then bring out the complete versions. To make more money, try putting only two or three episodes on each tape. Alternatively, film some inexpensive extra footage – or gather some off the cutting room floor – and hike up the price of what you can now call a 'special release'.

8: When *Doctor Who* is next cancelled, establish a fund to sue the BBC for its reinstatement, then find yourself unable to use the money for any such thing.

9: Write a factual book: some knowledge of the programme is useful but not essential. If you do get everything wrong, you can make more cash by bringing out a volume of corrections. For best results, stick in a few photographs and jack up the price by two hundred per cent.

10: Start a publishing company and release as many *Doctor Who* titles as you can cram on to the shelves.

DILDO, THE PLANET: Amusing misprint in *The Doctors – Thirty Years of Time Travel* book.

DINOSAURS: The outward appearance of these prehistoric monsters is still the subject of much speculation. Although palaeontologists have painstakingly recreated complete skeletons from fossilised remains, their true fleshed-out look is, with few exceptions, a matter for conjecture. With this in mind, who is to say that the creatures seen in 'Invasion of the Dinosaurs' were any less realistic than those in *Jurassic Park*? See also PAPIER-MÂCHÉ PUPPETS.

DISNEY TIME: The Tom Baker-hosted episode of this cartoon-clip anthology show made an unprecedented bid for *Doctor Who* canonicity by having a disembodied hand pass Baker a request for help from the Brigadier on Earth. This dovetailed nicely into the new season's opener, 'Terror of the Zygons' (although, for realism and the ability to frighten, the Skarasen fails to compare with Mickey and Pluto). Of course, it conflicts with the scenario presented in 'Revenge of the Cybermen', so you'd have to imagine that that story never occurred. Not a problem, we think.

DISRESPECTFUL USAGE OF THE COPY-RIGHTED TARDIS DEVICE: See the cover.

'DOCTOR BONK': Why did fans become so irate following tabloid speculation that the movie Doctor, played by Donald Sutherland that week, was to get to grips with Caroline Munro (chance would be a fine thing)? Or, more recently, that the eighth Doctor was to be more than friendly with Grace Holloway? Were they concerned that it was out of character for the Doctor, a timeless near-immortal being, aware of the ephemeral fragility of the human species, to let himself become too emotionally involved with a woman, knowing he would one day have to endure the pain of watching her wither and die while he remained the same (just like that Highlander bloke)? Or were they simply afraid that they'd no longer be able to identify with their hero if he got to shag a girl, because they never would?

DOCTORIN' THE TARDIS: There is one school of thought which contends that the seventh Doctor spent the gap between being powerful and enigmatic in 'Survival' and getting swiftly killed off in 'The US Telemovie with the Pertwee Logo' having all those New Adventures. Actually, it's perfectly obvious that all that time was spent giving the TARDIS a complete make-over. *The Doctor Who Movie Special* published by Marvel gives some interesting insights into the refurbished TARDIS, especially the new console. Apparently it is set upon an energised control platform sensitive to all lifeforms and programmed to only respond to beings with human ancestry. Very useful on a Gallifreyan vessel! The Holographic Scanner Control, which shows an image of the ship's surroundings, would have proved even more useful had the Doctor bothered to look at it instead of walking straight out into a hail of bullets.

DOCTOR WHO – **A CELEBRATION:** The BBC's own twentieth anniversary event, held in the grounds of Longleat House (see LONGLEAT) over Easter Weekend 1983. It gave fans an unparalleled opportunity to stand in lots of queues and catch glimpses of distant celebrities. Messages had to be put out on the radio to warn people not to think of travelling there on Bank Holiday Monday, as the place was heaving (now go and read 'SCIENCE-FICTION ISN'T POPULAR' and see if it doesn't make you seethe with impotent fury). As well as the event, the name was used for a concurrent W H Allen book – the first of many near-identical volumes penned by Peter Haining.

'DOCTOR WHO AND THE HELL PLANET': Exciting, if a little short, 'Missing Adventure' by Terrance Dicks, published in the *Daily Mirror*. The fourth Doctor lands on a prehistoric world where he has a bit of a tough time with natural disasters and dinosaurs. The surprise ending reveals the Hell Planet in question to be none other than . . . Earth! Big shock, we don't think. The biggest surprise would have been for this tale to have taken place anywhere in the universe except Earth.

DOCTOR WHO **APPRECIATION SOCIETY (DWAS):** Long-standing official fan club, almost popularised by television's *That's Life*. For the most dedicated of the Time Lord's followers, the Society boasts a monthly newsletter, *Celestial Toyroom*, which has been known to turn up in the month mentioned on the cover. To reflect the international scope of its membership, the DWAS holds its annual conventions in such diverse locations as Coventry and, erm, Coventry.

***DOCTOR WHO* FANDOM, PUBLIC IMAGES OF:**
It's a sad fact that the media have always failed to understand why anyone should be interested in their own products. Their angle on *Doctor Who*-related news, then, is always likely to be the insane, dribbling reactions of the most pathetic group of anoraked devotees they can find. In a convention hall packed with five hundred sensibly dressed people and one in a Leela costume, you know where the TV crews will head. And, for the rest of us, there's no use in fighting this stereotype. It doesn't matter how much of a dignified front you put on: around the next corner, there's always a Scarf-Wearing Fanatical Whovian Bastard who'll ruin things by dressing as a Vervoid and parading himself in front of the cameras, or doing one of the things on the accompanying list . . .

TEN TRIED AND TRUSTED WAYS OF BRINGING FANDOM INTO DISREPUTE

1: Invite a television crew into your merchandise-festooned bedroom and agree to dress up as a character from the series. For best results, pick one to whom you bear no resemblance whatsoever.

2: Appear on TV to slag off the programme's writers for their scientific inaccuracy and structural incohesion.

3: When a journalist/presenter makes an off-the-cuff quip about the Daleks' inability to tackle staircases, take pains to point out that that was all changed in 'Remembrance' and that, anyway, they must have climbed stairs to get on to the deck of the *Mary Celeste* (sic) in 'The Chase', so there.

4: Get on to a phone-in programme and ask the producer of *Doctor Who* if he created the new title sequence on a BBC Micro.

5: Admit on live TV that your earliest memories are not of your parents, but of the Daleks.

6: Reveal that you've named your children after the

Doctor's companions. Ben and Polly or Ian and Barbara will do, but for that extra humiliation factor, try Adric and Nyssa.

7: Express your annoyance about *Doctor Who*'s eighteen-month suspension by putting your foot through a television screen. Invite the papers around to photograph the evidence.

8: Proclaim yourself to be a normal person with a natural hobby, then, when pressed, recite your favourite lines from classic episodes in a funny voice.

9: Phone your local radio station to claim that your wheelie bin has been making wheezing, groaning sounds and must therefore be a TARDIS in disguise.

10: Bind your lover in chains, then plug him into the mains in a jealousy-motivated murder attempt. When asked about your crime later, claim to be the chairman of the *Doctor Who* Fan Club. This need not be true, so long as it makes for a good headline.

DOCTOR WHO – JOURNEY THROUGH TIME: Published in the USA in 1985, this large hardcover book featured material from World Distributors annuals and for once actually deigned to credit some of the writers (Charles Pemberton, Lesley Scott and Brenda Apsley – although with Brenda Apsley also holding the editorial reins, that's perhaps not surprising). The book was a reprint of the UK *Doctor Who Special* published by Galley, which in turn was a partial reprint of an earlier World annuals reprint compilation with some additional fifth and sixth Doctor reprints chucked in. As far as we can ascertain, *Doctor Who – Journey Through Time* did not make it on to the bestseller lists.

DOCTOR WHO ON THE PLANET ZACTUS: A first Doctor adventure so nail-bitingly exciting that it had to be published in the form of a painting book to suppress the potentially heart-stopping tension.

DOCTOR WHO TELEMOVIE, UNUSED SCRIPTS

FOR: Didn't we all breathe a sigh of relief when we learnt that the McGann feature was to follow established TV continuity? (Didn't we all breathe a sigh of relief when we learnt that the bloody thing was really going to happen?) A quick perusal of early versions however, reveals that this wasn't always the case.* First mooted as a pilot for an ongoing series, an early draft envisaged the Doctor as a Time Lord equivalent of an old-style British explorer, reminiscent of Richard Burton (no, not the Welsh one who was always marrying Liz Taylor), who is on a quest to find his missing father. Back on Gallifrey, the Master is Prime Minister, while the Doctor's Grandfather, Borusa (well naturally, grumpy old Mr Who, right?), is Lord President. Davros and the Daleks were to be in it too, as invaders of the Time Lords' home world – what's the betting that a huge chunk of the budget would have gone on a Gallifrey set? Had it gone ahead, presumably Brad Pitt would have appeared as Davros, without make-up, with Jean-Claude Van Damme cast as Borusa. Remember how it took the fourth Doctor all of Season Sixteen (or one entire eight-page comic strip in *Doctor Who Magazine*) to gather the segments of the Key to Time? Well another outline, for a two-parter, was submitted in which he finds them all in episode one. Apparently this haste is because he needs them to defeat none other than Zodin – sounds terrible.

* This 'information' came via someone we know slightly who has access to the internet. Therefore we make no apologies for the distinct possibility that it may be all lies.

DODD, KEN: Tattifilarious buck-toothed comedian from Knotty Ash whose discomknockerating perform-ance in 'Delta and the Bannermen' fitted perfectly into the style of Season Twenty-four. Speaks volumes really, doesn't it? How tickled we weren't. See also CON-TROVERSIAL USE OF STAR CELEBRITIES IN PREFERENCE TO PROPER ACTORS.

DODO: Affectionate name for Dorothea Chaplet, a companion of the first Doctor. Virgin Publishing have been slightly less affectionate towards her, establishing via two different writers that she left the TARDIS with a terminal disease (sexually transmitted, of course – this was a Virgin *Doctor Who* book!), then had her head blown off by a mad gunman. Hence, presumably, the phrase 'As dead as a Dodo'.

DOUBLE ENTENDRES, SO-CALLED: Sub-sections of entries in *The Discontinuity Guide*, which we feel marred an otherwise excellent publication.* The authors seemed to be under the impression that if a line of dialogue included the word 'end', 'come', or even 'act', it was worthy of a place in one of Talbot Rothwell's classic *Carry On* scripts. Not so. However, in their quest for these 'amusing' quotes, they did come across (fnur fnur) a couple of nice ones (oo-er) and, not being averse to the odd bit of smut ourselves (hoo hoo), we felt the urge (yuk yuk) to likewise whip out (chortle) some of our own. 'I'm going down, even if you're not'; 'Get a hold of this pole. Take it over that side. Make room for me. Right, you ready? Then off we go'; 'Now what?', 'We go up this crevasse.' Sadly, after a few minutes, we got bored, turned off 'The Green Death' part three and got on with something more interesting.

* *Although their assertion that 'Dimensions in Time' followed directly after 'Shada' in canonical* Doctor Who *chronology was bollocks too.*

50

DOUBLES: Considering the sheer vastness of space and time, it's just a bit of a coincidence that the Doctor frequently runs into people who are identical to either himself or his travelling companions (not to mention sundry android replicas, parallel universe counterparts, cacti, etc). Presumably he became so used to this happening that when he met Lexa (in 'Meglos'), he didn't feel compelled to exclaim something along the lines of 'Oi, you're a dead ringer for Barbara Wright y'know!'

DOWNTIME: Appropriately titled video spin-off: if you spent seventeen quid on its initial release, chances are you'd feel pretty down by the time you'd watched it. It was better value at £10.99, though, especially with appearances by the Brig and Sarah Jane. There was someone called Victoria in it too; but, although Debbie Watling played her, she was quite bright and didn't scream all the time so it couldn't have been our Victoria. The video was a sort of follow-up to the much less ambitious *Wartime*, which just featured Benton. Don't mock though, at least it had a *Doctor Who* character in it. *Shakedown* (do all these things have to have 'down' or 'time' in the title?) had both Carole Ann Ford and Sophie Aldred in the cast but, for copyright reasons, neither was allowed to play their *Doctor Who* role. Even the Sontarans had face lifts just in case. It all gets much more confusing in the PROBE series. Liz Shaw is always meeting people identical to various Doctors and companions and is completely ignorant of the fact. It was a bit much when she met that bloke played by Jon Pertwee and never noticed. At this rate, her investigative outfit will soon be out of business.

DRACULA: The Prince of Darkness, Lord of the Undead, a terrifying creature of nightmare with strong sexual undertones attached to his nocturnal feeding habits. So quite why the organisers of the Festival of Ghana in the far-flung future world of 1996 chose to represent him as an overweight, brylcreem-haired, unattractive kind of guy in their 'House of Horrors' exhibit is unclear. Have these people never heard of Christopher Lee? Their Frankenstein Monster was crap too.

DRAHVINS: Race of evil blonde babes who sadly never returned to threaten the Doctor after their encounter in 'Galaxy 4'. But had the series ever taken off in America, well they'd have been a cert.

DREDLOX, THE: Metallic monsters with a distinctive battle cry of 'In-cin-er-ate!' They first appeared in the American Marvel comic *Power Man and Iron Fist* issue 79, cover dated March 1982, along with their arch-foe Professor Gamble. Gamble was a Victorian gentleman whose bookshop was bigger on the inside than the outside, and later dematerialised. At the time, we thought there was something a wee bit familiar about all this, so we were indebted to the 'Gallifrey Guardian' section of *Doctor Who Monthly* for pointing out what it was. Apparently, the working title for 'City of Death' was 'A Gamble with Time'! Well, how did they get away with such a blatant rip-off as that?! Things became more bizarre when Marvel USA, refusing as always to let a bad character die, brought back both Gamble and the Dredlox over a decade later in a story which was actually called 'A Gamble with Time', in the back of *Avengers Annual* issue 22. 'Dredlox' was obviously considered too old-fashioned a name, though, and the creatures were rechristened 'Incinerators'. This tale features a meeting between Professor Gamble and Merlin, so we think it must be a reference to the TV adventure 'Battlefield'.

DR WHO ANNUAL 1972, THE: Forget the mystery of the *Marie* (or *Mary*, or whatever she was bloody well called) *Celeste* (which may be difficult due to the alarming frequency with which it turns up in these pages): a real puzzle to ponder over is the truly baffling lack of this item of Pertwee memorabilia from the World Distributors Christmas 1971 output. Perhaps they'd run out of space-related trivia to impart.

'DR WHO IS REQUIRED. BRING HIM HERE': Simple request from WOTAN that has subsequently become the source of much controversy within fandom. Dr Who indeed. Believe it or not, there have even been attempts to explain away this erroneous piece of scripting, by far the silliest being that Who is the Doctor's real name. The only possible explanation for the mistake would be that the loony computer had a copy of *TV Comic* delivered each week to the Post Office Tower.

E

'EACH SCREAMING GIRL JUST HOPED THAT A YETI WOULDN'T SHOOT 'ER': Touching line from 'Doctor in Distress', culminating in an inspired rhyme for 'canine computer'. See the accompanying chart rundown.

THE *DOCTOR WHO* TOP TEN

10: 'I'm Gonna Spend My Christmas with a Dalek' by The Go Gos (presumably with a very young Belinda Carlisle). A truly dreadful, wince-making, vomit-inducing track. But still better than most of the others on this list.

9: 'Doctor Who' by Mankind. A disco version of the *Who* theme. Yeah, right. But it's got a good beat.

8: 'Who's Who' by Roberta Tovey. Ostensibly a film spin-off, yet the lyrics refer to 'a man with long grey hair', and of course Peter Cushing's hair in the movies was rather short. Now, William Hartnell sported long white hair, so we seem to have a combination of the two characters. In our opinion, young Roberta was striving to reconcile the *Who* universes with this well-meaning, bridge-building song of peace.

7: 'Who's Dr Who' by Frazer Hines. Frazer thought the popularity of Jamie would help him to achieve an ambition of pop-stardom. The record-buying public thought otherwise.

6: 'Who is the Doctor' by Jon Pertwee. Jon might well have crossed the void beyond the mind on this record, but at least he didn't attempt to sing.

5: 'Dr Who is Gonna Fix it' by Bulamakanka. It would be easy to dismiss this record as a pile of bulamakak, but we mustn't be too harsh. Taking into account the fact that the band came from Australia – the land that gave us such rock luminaries as Kylie and Jason, Rolf Harris and INXS – it's likely that Bulamakanka were the pinnacle of Oz-rock.

4: 'Landing of the Daleks' by the Earthlings. The BBC banned the original version of this record due to its morse code message warning of the imminent arrival of invaders from Skaro. Quite right too: someone conversant with morse may have heard it and assumed that the popular outer space robot people from television's *Doctor Who* really had landed on Earth.

3: 'Doctor . . .?' by Blood Donor. A genuine novelty this one: a *Doctor Who* inspired number that's actually rather good.

2: 'Doctor in Distress' by Who Cares. We imagine the Doctor was in distress because he'd heard this record. Released during the cancellation crisis, this charity disc had been announced as an epic of Band Aid proportions, featuring a host of pop megastars. As it turned out, they got Sally Thomsett from *Man About the House*. The BBC refused to play it, either because it embarrassed them by harping on about the suspension of *Doctor Who*, or because it was crap. Take your pick. Although a flop in chart terms, the record did achieve its aims: rather than risk Who Cares doing a follow-up, the BBC commissioned Season Twenty-three.

1: 'Doctorin' the TARDIS' by The Time Lords. We're putting this in the number one spot because it actually reached that esteemed position. Imagine that: a *Doctor Who* related disc topping the UK charts. See Frazer, it can be done!

EARTH: 27th-century winners of the Intergalactic Olympic Games.

EDMONDS, NOEL: When part two of 'Dimensions in Time' aired during an episode of *Noel's House Party*, the eponymous host had the good sense to order it cut down to size. Thus viewers were spared two extra minutes of puerile, mindless *Doctor Who*, and were treated instead to more celebrities being covered in gunge, sportsmen scrabbling for money in a wind tank, and national megastar Mr Blobby falling over in a variety of hilarious ways.

ENCYCLOPEDIA OF THE WORLDS OF DOCTOR WHO, THE: Excellent and comprehensive reference work that alphabetically lists every person, location and gadget to appear in *Doctor Who*, right up to the letter 'S'. There was one blatant omission, though, hence:

CASTROVALVA: Big city in which the Doctor got lost.

Now all you need is a pair of scissors and some glue, and your book is finally complete. You will, of course, then have to rush out and buy another copy of this one, as yours will have a big hole in it. Still, it's worth it for the peace of mind, isn't it?

'ENEMY WITHIN, THE': Semi-official title for the McGann movie. So why didn't they stick it on screen, then we wouldn't have to go around calling it 'Doctor Who – The Almost-an-Hour-and-a-Half Telemovie'? 'The Enemy Within' was also the working title for 'The Android Invasion' and 'The Invisible Enemy', and an unused fifth Doctor story by Christopher Priest. One of these days, this persistent name is bound to find its way on to an actual episode. It's only fair.

ENGLISH: Universal language of all people, even those from Ancient Rome or Revolutionary France.

Taking a leaf from the fifth *Doctor Who* annual, 'The Masque of Mandragora' finally mentioned that this was a 'Time Lord gift', thereby allowing us to gloss over the whole vexed question. Well, it's better than subtitles, innit? See TARDIS TELEPATHIC CIRCUITS for another inadequate explanation.

EOCENE: Yet another era of Earth's pre-history from which the Silurians probably didn't originate.

ERGON: Giant chicken that threatened the fifth Doctor in Amsterdam.

EVIL SINCE THE DAWN OF TIME: Perhaps the Doctor's most powerful enemy, the consummately evil Fenric was able to transport Ace across four dimensions to Iceworld, allow Lady Peinforte's free movement through the timestream, bring the future Haemovores to the present, and ruthlessly manipulate the lives of generations of Earthlings. Fortunately, he was a sucker for a good game of chess and could rarely bring himself to conquer and pillage whilst in a losing position. Would that all power-hungry megalomaniacs could be so easily distracted . . .

Davros: My Dalek machines will make me invincible!

Doctor: Yes, yes, but first, how about a game of Ludo?

Davros: Bugger it, I've rolled a one. I'll never get round to my galactic domination at this rate!

EYEPATCH JOKE, THE: The story of an amusing prank played during the making of 'Inferno', this epitomises that collection of behind-the-scenes anecdotes which are wheeled out at every *Doctor Who* convention and have thus achieved near-legendary status. It isn't the fault of the actors concerned, of course. What else can you do when confronted with a question from the floor like 'Did anything funny happen to you during filming?' or 'Were any tricks played on you, involving eyepatches?'

TEN ENDURING CONVENTION ANECDOTES
(EDITED HIGHLIGHTS)

1: 'I shot out into the hall, wearing just my knickers, and who should walk in but the vicar!'

2: 'We had knickers instead of hankies. "They're not mine!" Debbie blushed.'

3: 'Pat came in and we were both wearing "Come Back Bill Hartnell" T-shirts.'

4: 'There was this naked German swimming nearby . . .'

5: 'She lifted up her arms and her boobs popped out!'

6: 'The glass cracked . . . I nearly died.'

7: '. . . Mr Jan Putrid . . .'

8: 'I sewed lead weights into the lining of my kilt . . .'

9: 'There was all this foam . . .'

10: '. . . but, when I turned around, they were all wearing eyepatches.'

F

FAN REACTION: One consequence of producing a cult programme is that its followers are liable to place every detail under the microscope. The makers of *EastEnders* can get away with changing Ian Beale's age for no good reason, and no one will pass comment (except that we just did), but JN-T allows the second Doctor to know his own future in 'The Five Doctors' and suddenly he's the Anti-Christ (see UNIT ADVENTURES, PROBLEMATIC TIME SCALE OF for proof that some writers will gleefully pick holes out of any old continuity mistake). As a rule, most magazines/fanzines will slag off all new *Who* for being cheap/pantomimesque/not real *Doctor Who*/unworthy of the diamond logo. The offending story will then be reviled for five or six years, after which it can be 're-evaluated'. At this point, its finer qualities will be retroactively appreciated, with favourable comparisons drawn to the current output, which will doubtless be cheap/pantomimesque/not real *Doctor Who*/unworthy of the diamond logo. This is, of course, half the fun of being a fan.

FANZINES: When videos were scarce, magazines few, and factual books numbered less than 20,000, fanzines were about the best way of keeping in touch with events and opinions. There were hundreds of the things, typically A5 and photocopied. The quality of the photos was not all it could have been, and let's face it, sometimes the writing was a bit shoddy and the artwork wouldn't have seemed out of place on a *Blake's 7* video cover. Buying a 'zine was a lottery – but then, they were always fun, made in the best of spirits, and some of them were (and still are) very good. Sadly for all fanzine editors past and present, a résumé of their successes would be dull, so we've decided to write a defamatory but more interesting list instead.

TEN SILLY THINGS THAT FANZINE EDITORS DO

1: They release slightly larger-than-normal editions and put two issue numbers on the front.

2: They run fan fiction in which, for example, five Doctors team up and are threatened by Sutekh, the Fendahl, the Valeyard and the Daleks.

3: They court legal action with headlines like 'JN-T MUST DIE!' Still, it gives them an edge over *Doctor Who Magazine*, doesn't it?

4: They feature interviews that consist of the hastily written responses of a celeb to a list of about six questions. Alternatively, their 'real' interviews focus more on how the meeting was arranged, how the writers (about six of them) travelled there, and so on, with actual quotations from the subject being scarce. A two-minute chat is therefore stretched over three issues (although, in fact, some 'professional' mags do this too).

5: They fail to appear for three months, then send subscribers a normal-sized issue with three dates on the front in the pretence that this will compensate.

6: They stick the first half of a two-part story in their first issue, little realising that 95 per cent of 'zines that follow this course are destined never to produce issue 2.

7: They run so-called event reports, in which the reviewer is less concerned with the specifics of the convention or whatever, and more with demonstrating what a great laddish bloke he was with his incredible hi-jinks throughout the day, and what bloody sad bastards the rest of the attendees were, as witness the fact that some of them actually stood in the autograph queue (next to him).

8: They run special offers for amazing free gifts, typically a piece of home-drawn artwork on an A4 piece of paper.

9: They produce fanzines devoted entirely to one actress, featuring reviews of her every performance, evaluations of her costumes, and unrequited love missives. Quite disturbing.

10: They save up enough money to fund a proper distribution network, then start to release a variety of periodicals and pretend to be real publishers.

FARRINGTON, IAN: Winner of a *TV Action* Design-a-Monster competition with his marvellous creation, the Uggrakks. For his efforts, he got a colour telly and the opportunity to see his monsters battle the third Doctor in comic strip form. If there'd been any justice, he would have landed a job at the BBC replacing those responsible for the Zarbi, War Machines, Krotons, silly monster in 'The Caves of Androzani', etc.

FAST-RETURN SWITCH: Useful TARDIS facility if you feel inclined to hurtle back to face certain death at the creation of the universe while the ship's telepathic circuits turn you into a psycho-killer. In all other respects, about as pointless as a mercury fluid link.

FEATURE PAGES: Unwarranted intrusions upon the World annuals, whose programme-related content faded ever more into the background against a plethora of facts along the lines of 'Did you know the sun's a bit hot?' Alongside pictures of astronauts and comparisons of planets to fruit sizes, the Doctor put in only brief appearances, usually trapped by malevolent number-puzzle fetishists or performing feats of telepathy that we could try at home if we were sad.

FENDLEMAN: Like many fictional villains, the Fendahl made one silly mistake. By naming its unwitting pawn 'Fendleman', it made it clear to everybody who the local 'man of the Fendahl' was. If all alien monsters were so stupid, UNIT's job would be much simpler. A quick look through a telephone directory and a round-up of all people with the surname 'Dalekagent' or 'Autonduplicate' would forestall most invasion attempts before they began.

FIFTH DOCTOR, THE: Too bland, too young and played as Tristan Farnon in space. That's how some people regarded Peter Davison's portrayal of the cricket-loving, celery-wearing TARDIS incumbent. But certainly not us.

FIRST FEMALE PRIME MINISTER, *DOCTOR WHO*'S UNCANNY PREDICTION OF THE : In the days before 'Mawdryn Undead' (see UNIT ADVENTURES, PROBLEMATIC TIMESCALE OF), fans used to be quietly pleased that 'Terror of the Zygons', with its near-future setting, had correctly guessed the unlikely gender of the next premier. It's all gone to pot now, of course, but we still feel bound to point out that this seeming flash of foresight was a drop in the ocean compared to the show's enormous number of palpable misses. Let's not forget that the PM before the unnamed female one was to be called Jeremy; that a race of cybernetic beings from a tenth planet were scheduled to invade in 1986; and that Letitia Dean was going to stay in *EastEnders* until 2003 (but see also FOWLER, ARTHUR).

FIZZADE: In the *Doctor Who* universe, a carbonated drink available from vending machines in Paradise Towers. In reality, various cans of pop with yellow labels stuck over familiar brand names and trademarks to give the impression of something new and interesting. The result was entirely convincing, however, and several years ago one can made an excellent auction item at Tencon in Liverpool. Or rather it would have done if the organisers hadn't insisted on getting it signed by a host of *Who* celebrities, no matter how tenuous their link with the aforementioned highrise. Was Sophie Aldred the companion in 'Paradise Towers'? No, it was bubbly Bonnie, wasn't it? Is Nick Courtney a man you associate with soft drinks? We don't think so. Why, oh why, do people assume that something becomes more valuable just because anyone from *Doctor Who* has scribbled their moniker on it? If collectors are so inclined they can go and get their stuff signed themselves! It's got so that guests now expect to have to sign everything that doesn't move. Convention organisers, please take note: the application of a little common sense is all that's required in auction situations. For example, if you have Anneke Wills and Michael Craze on your guest list, get them to sign a copy of the Target *Tenth Planet* book, hang on to it for a year or two, and at your next event you'll have a nice desirable item for sale. However, if you also happen to have an original 'Tenth Planet' Cyberman costume in pristine condition up for grabs, do not, repeat do not hand Mike and Anneke a black marker pen and say 'Here, you two, write an amusing message on this old thing, would you? It'll fetch an extra few bob.' Because it won't.

FLAT, CIRCULAR FEET: A physical characteristic peculiar to the Sensorites. It is remarkable that the inhabitants of the Sense Sphere were able to attain their advanced evolutionary state. On other worlds, you would expect beings hindered by such ungainly appendages to trip and fall themselves into extinction before leaving their caves.

FLESH TIME: Ha, we thought you'd buck up a bit when you spotted this one. Sorry to disappoint, though, it's merely the term the Urbankans used to describe their pre-android state. So nothing to do with shagging at all. Boring, eh?

FLORANA: One of the most beautiful vacation spots in the galaxy, or so we're led to believe. The Doctor was en route to this planet with Sarah Jane when he took an enforced detour to Exxilon for yet another run-in with the dreaded Daleks (he won again, if you're interested). That he never reached Florana is probably for the best: on a BBC budget, this exquisite world would no doubt have been interpreted as a sand pit with a few plastic flowers strewn about. Just look at the much-vaunted Eye of Orion, which ended up resembling Wales on a wet weekend.

FOOTBALL: Some people think that *Who* fans would be better off if they took an interest in football instead (as if the two hobbies are mutually exclusive). We don't see much difference. Soccer fans spend Saturday afternoons watching their heroes struggle against opposition, with most contests lasting about ninety minutes. Alternatively, they pore over and memorise statistics, or put on long scarves to attend gatherings of like-minded people, where they can see their idols in the flesh. And if you want to talk about dressing up, try comparing sales of *Doctor Who* T-shirts with those of Man United. At least when the Doctor loses, his supporters don't go out and beat the crap out of anyone who cheered for the Daleks, and to the best of our knowledge no one has ever been kung-fu kicked by a convention guest, whether they deserved it or not.

FOREIGN LOCATIONS: There were always good aesthetic and logistical reasons for recording *Doctor Who* abroad, and the fact that all the locations chosen were popular tourist spots was incidental. It did mean, however, that when the Doctor visited foreign climes, we could expect a good long outdoor chase scene to show off the expensive surroundings (although he is probably the only person ever to have spent twenty minutes dashing around Amsterdam without once passing a retail outlet for drugs, vibrators, or a good time). Most effective of all these settings was probably Lanzarote, which, when it doubled for the planet of fire, Sarn, made a nice change from the usual woods and quarries. When it also doubled for Lanzarote, however, it was a bit of a giveaway, and one had to wonder why Peri thought she had been taken to a different world at all. The following year, Spain became the show's final exotic destination; Season Twenty-three's suspension forced the abandonment of a planned jaunt to Singapore, for which a justification was being hastily scripted. Budget cuts subsequently confined the production team to a week at Butlin's. And no, we haven't forgotten McGann's trip to Canada, it's just that under the circumstances it doesn't really count, does it?

FOREMAN, I M: Erm . . . pass.

FOREMAN, SUSAN: The existence of this character is a thorn in the side of *Doctor Who* historians. Her claim to be the Time Lord's granddaughter runs contrary to fandom's accepted view of the Doctor as a

67

man without reproductive organs, or at least without an interest in employing them. Eric Saward addressed this knotty problem in the *Radio Times Twentieth Anniversary Special*; his short story, 'Birth of a Renegade', established that Susan was in fact the Lady Larn, the only living descendant of Rassilon (nobody minds if he had sex), who called her travelling partner 'Grandfather' as a term of endearment. But was this tale canonical? Could Susan have been a Time Lady at all? There's no evidence of children on Gallifrey, and her claim to have created the name 'TARDIS' is clearly an outright lie. Furthermore, the Doctor would have been unlikely to condone her marriage to David Campbell, knowing that the age difference would eventually prove insurmountable. So there you have it. Was Susan the Doctor's granddaughter or not? We don't care.

FOREWORD BY PHILIP HINCHCLIFFE: Amusing omission from the book *Classic Who – The Hinchcliffe Years*.

FOWLER, ARTHUR: Having been granted permission to incorporate *EastEnders* continuity into 'Dimensions in Time', John Nathan-Turner and David Roden took the huge and unwarranted liberty of killing off this popular character. How would they like it if the death of, say, Sarah Jane Smith was mentioned in passing at the Queen Vic?

FOWLER, ARTHUR [addendum]: Blimey, since the above was written *EastEnders*'ve gone and killed 'im off. So, once again, *Doctor Who*'s predictions of our future world have proved to be spookily accurate. See also the accompanying list.

TEN SOAP OPERA CROSSOVERS THAT WOULD HAVE BEEN MORE ENTERTAINING THAN 'DIMENSIONS IN TIME'

1: *Coronation Street*. Hilariously retitled *Terrynation Street*, or even *The Tribe of Ee Bah Gum*, this would have had the Doctor landing in Salford and meeting loads of past associates, all in disguise. It would have featured Marco Polo, Ian Chesterton, Mary Ashe, Jack Tyler and more.

2: *Emmerdale.* Or *Emmerdalek*, as we like to think it would have been called. Joe Sugden returns from the dead, played by Hamish Wilson.

3: *The Young Doctors*. Prequel to the first episode, featuring all seven Doctors as Time Tots. Recasting would have had to take place, of course, but we would at least have been spared the sight of those heads whizzing around the Rani's TARDIS.

4: *Brookside*. The Doctor, the TARDIS, Daleks, etc, could have been incorporated into this programme without compromising its realism one bit.

5: *Dallas.* Likewise, the concepts of regeneration and returns from the dead would be right at home here. Perhaps the fourth Doctor could come round under that radio telescope thing, relieved that the last eight seasons had all been a dreadful nightmare (though wasn't that the proposed plot of 'The Dark Dimension'?).

6: *Prisoner: Cell Block H.* Wobbly walls, endless corridor sets, characters being put in cells every two minutes . . . This is practically *Doctor Who* already.

7: *Revelations.* 'Revelations of the Daleks', redone with sex and bishops. This was probably the inspiration for Paul Cornell's first New Adventure.

8: *Crossroads.* This too has been done, to some extent, with 'The Trial of a Time Lord', which, like *Crossroads*, went on forever even though the viewers hated it.

9: *Grange Hill.* 'Remembrance of the Daleks' almost did it, but didn't quite dare to make it official. See BRONSON, MISTER.

10: *EastEnders.* Yes, even this could have been lots better, if only the writers had realised the potential of having

Ian Reddington as a current member of the soap's cast. Imagine the impact of a cliffhanger in which 'Tricky Dicky' Cole pulls back a latex mask to reveal . . . the Chief Clown! Ratings would have soared.

FRANKLIN'S BOW WOWS: Mid-eighties fan club for those *Doctor Who* fans who found themselves enchanted to the point of tears by Richard Franklin's rendition of 'Daddy Wouldn't Buy Me a Bow Bow', or were simply impressed by his macho posturing in the guise of Captain Yates. Members had the opportunity to go on trips with like-minded individuals and raise money for canine charities. They also received a badge with a big bone on it.

FREAK LOCALISED WEATHER CONDITIONS: Script addition stand-by, useful for when the film crew turns up at a location to finish scenes begun the previous day in brilliant sunshine, only to find that it's snowing a blizzard. It's a pity someone didn't offer a similar excuse in 'Silver Nemesis', a story clearly stated as taking place on 23 November but obviously filmed in the middle of Summer.

G

GALAXY 5: Not in fact a sequel to 'Galaxy 4', but the Federation's opponents in a big galactic war (not that a galactic war could be anything other than big).

GALLIFREYAN HIGH COUNCIL, CONTINUAL INCIDENCES OF MADNESS AND TREACHERY AMONGST THE: When is somebody going to think of another Gallifrey-based plotline?

GAMES: What could be more satisfying for the true enthusiast than to re-enact the Doctor's greatest battles in the safety and comfort of home? From the programme's earliest days, successive merchandisers have tried to fulfil this desire, and, inasmuch as the Doctor ever beat the Daleks by rolling dice and moving counters around a board, they have succeeded. The accompanying list details some of the main games available, although we have chosen to neglect the fascinating tests of skill and judgement that appeared in the World Distributors annuals. For the most part, these were the same game anyway, redrawn with pictures of different characters – some from *Doctor Who* – in the background. See also COMPUTER GAMES.

TEN NOTABLE *DOCTOR WHO* GAMES

1: 'Dodge the Daleks'. An early attempt, in which the object of the game is to dodge some Daleks. Nostalgic and intriguing though it sounds, it's actually simplistic enough to be one of World's efforts (except that an even lower-budget version – 'Dodge the Dalek' in the Souvenir Press *Dalek Book* – got there first).

2: 'The Great Escape'. One of those 3-D maze things where you have to get the ball across the board without it falling down holes. However – and this is the interesting bit – it has some Daleks drawn on it.

3: 'The *Doctor Who* Board Game'. The name of this seventies product says it all. It's about *Doctor Who* and it's played on a board. Some nice additions, such as a topless plastic TARDIS (oo-er), raise it above the level of its predecessors.

4: 'War of the Daleks'. More state-of-the-art than anything before it. This features a great big three-dimensional Emperor Dalek in the middle of the board. Turn the Emperor and its army of little silver and gold Daleks rotates to cut off the players. Sheer brilliance – or it would be, if it worked.

5: The Weetabix Game. Probably the most exciting piece of merchandise since the first Weetabix giveaway. This time, the inevitable free character cards (depicting Bellal, Vega Nexas and other great adversaries) were designed to slot into four fantastic game boards, which could be used separately or stuck together to form one huge playing surface with Gallifrey at the centre. Hours of fun.

6: *Doctor Who* Trump Cards. Just about everything was reduced to a Top Trumps set in the seventies, but the *Doctor Who* game is novel in that half its cards have nothing to do with the programme. Historical figures are pitted against alien monsters, some of which provide additional entertainment by having absurd attributes or the wrong illustrations. Plenty of fun to be had here by pitting, say, Annie Oakley against the Ogrons (although she'd have to sort them out from the Sea Devils first), or working out which of the Doctor's chums have been picked up from Earth and which from the Land of Fiction. Interestingly, the Daleks don't appear, which hints at copyright problems. Davros and the Mechanoids, however, do. Is it too late for Terry Nation to sue?

7: *Doctor Who* (Games Workshop board game). An intriguing and complex strategy game that has one large drawback. It takes all day to deal the teetering stacks of cardboard discs to each square, and only one sneeze to end the game prematurely. Lots of fun to be had, though, chortling at the likenesses on the companions' tokens, particularly 'Susie'.

8: 'The *Doctor Who* Role-Playing Game' (FASA). Another fad that borrowed the series' name. Like many RPGs, this was workable but sometimes cumbersome. If you couldn't stretch to the task of imagining the whole adventure, you could buy some nice but expensive figures of *Doctor Who* characters to stimulate your mind's eye.

9: *Doctor Who – Timelord* (Virgin). Some years after the original role-playing game, Peter Darvill-Evans and Ian Marsh devised an entirely different system, contained in one book. This was an absolutely brilliant and flawless concept, although as Peter happens to be one of our editors, he'll probably alter our comments.

10: 'Battle for the Universe'. Inevitably, a *Doctor Who* game was going to be complete dross, and this is it. However, the subtle alteration in the Key to Time – so that it resembles the Key to Someone's Front Door – provides a second or two's jollity.

GARM: Large anthropomorphic dog that landed a job on Terminus.

GENTLY, DIRK: Literary character created by Douglas Adams. His adventures, the cynical amongst us might say, bore some resemblance to those of a certain Doctor. The appearance of a Professor Chronotis, for example, was a bit of a giveaway, as was Gently's use of whole portions of Romana's dialogue. In the writer's defence, he probably considered 'Shada' an unused script, unaware that hordes of fans had procured the completed material from the BBC archives and practically treated it as canonical. And, incidentally, there's no excuse for re-using the plot to 'City of Death'.

GIRL ILLUSTRATED: The magazine in which curvy Katy Manning famously bared all (issue 7, for any perverts who might be reading). She appeared in several more gratuitous poses than most people realise: the same one has been chosen constantly to represent the whole spread, presumably appealing to fans as it shows none of Katy's rude bits but does feature a Dalek.

<hr />

NINE *DOCTOR WHO* STARS WHO'VE BARED ALL (OR CERTAIN BITS) FOR THEIR ART, AND ONE WHO HASN'T

1: Debbie Watling, most notably in *Danger UXB*, but more commonly spotted in *That'll be the Day*, with David Essex giving them a helping hand out of her bra.

2: Wendy Padbury, in the early-seventies horror pic *Blood on Satan's Claw*. But it's rather brief, so you may need to keep a finger of your free hand on the video's pause button.

3: Katy Manning, as detailed above. Right then, how many of you sad pervs out there are going to admit to having a copy? And, more importantly, is anyone prepared to sell?

4: Elisabeth Sladen. Blink and you'll miss a shot of the left one in the Granada series *Send in the Girls*.

5: Louise Jameson got 'em out in *Tenko*. But didn't everybody?

6: Lalla Ward went topless in an early film role. Several years later, the public service magazine *Club International* considerately printed the stills. They also published photos purporting to show Lalla's front bottom, although the disembodied shots could have been of anyone's, and Lalla successfully proved in court that it wasn't hers. Just how she managed that, we wouldn't like to speculate.

7: Janet Fielding in a stage production of *The Warp*, apparently. That's not much good, is it? We need video evidence.

8: Nicola Bryant – the odd one out. She turned down wadges of cash to appear in the altogether in a men's magazine. Strange, because the next best thing happened all the time. You only have to look at the *Companions* book (not the John Nathan-Turner one).

9: Kate O'Mara has displayed her charms on several occasions, as collectors of *Club International* will no doubt be aware. And why not? It's perfectly acceptable for serious actresses to appear nude if they consider such scenes integral to the plot and not merely gratuitous titillation. No doubt Kate thought it was essential to appear topless on the publicity posters when she played Cleopatra a few years back. It was classical theatre, after all.

10: We're reliably informed that Sylvester McCoy had his tackle on display in the stage production of *Having a Ball* but, quite honestly, we couldn't care less. The same applies to Ian Marter's nude scenes in some film or other.

———◆———

GOLD: The problem with scary, invincible monsters like the Cybermen is that it's hard to get rid of them credibly by the end of part four. 'Revenge of the Cybermen' tackled this problem by giving the cyborg villains an unexpected weakness. Gold, apparently, clogs their chestplates and enough of it can kill them. Fair enough. But successive writers couldn't leave it there: by 1988, gold had become the Cybermen's equivalent of a vampire's garlic. Sadly, monsters are neither scary nor invincible if you can destroy them by bouncing coins off their chest units and then watching sixteen of them explode. It's fortunate that the series ended when it did, as the logical progression of Cyber development would have seen the monsters fleeing in terror from Spandau Ballet concerts and being unable to walk into a bank without prolapsing.

GOLD DALEK: Despite the fact that the budget for 'Day of the Daleks' stretched to only three of the eponymous creatures, somebody had the bright idea of painting one gold. This totally ruined the scenes in which an alien army attacked Sir Reginald Styles's house: their pronounced deficiency in the Dalek department was a good fifty per cent more obvious than it had to be. Still, at least they made the effort, which is more than you can say for a certain more recent episode.

GOLD, SIR KEITH: Inferno Project director, and potentially the Cybermen's greatest enemy.

GOODIES: No, we aren't going to write about Bill, Graeme and Tim, even if their show did feature guest appearances by Pat Troughton and Jon Pertwee and a flypast by the TARDIS. Of more significance is the confectionery company of the same name, which brought *Doctor Who* related comestibles to the public for over a decade. After a humble start distributing Cadet's sweet cigarettes, they worked their way up to producing their own penny chews with a distinctly *Doctor Who*-ish flavour (well, with pictures of *Doctor Who* characters on their wrappers, anyway). Their finest triumph, however, was a collection of white-chocolate slabs, which came in four shapes: Dalek, Cyberman, TARDIS and K9. These first appeared in the late seventies, but could still be purchased in 1982, making them the world's longest-running items of edible *Who* merchandise. Even that's a long time ago now, though, which poses a problem for anyone who collected them. Let's face it: nice as it may be to have the whole item, it's hardly in mint condition any more. On the other hand, those of us who bowed to the inevitable and scoffed the things found that the packaging, carefully re-wrapped about cardboard, made for some pretty nifty tree decorations at Christmas. The chocolate tasted pretty good too – but if you didn't discover that at the time, we wouldn't advise you to investigate at this late stage.

GREEL, MAGNUS: Proprietor of a butcher's shop in Brisbane, Australia.

H

HADRON ENERGY: According to the script for 'Castrovalva', the Master used 'hadron' energy to bind Adric. Judging by its visible effect on the lad, however, we suspect a slight misprint.

HALF-HUMAN: The contribution to the *Doctor Who* mythos by the makers of 'The US Telemovie with the Pertwee Logo', and judging by the eighth Doctor's interest in Grace Holloway, it's the bottom half. But come on, really, why would he hide the fact for over thirty years and then go round telling everyone he meets whether they care or not? It's Philip Segal's theory that the Doctor's father, by a strange coincidence, was exiled to Earth by the Time Lords, whereupon he met and did the business with the Doctor's mother. Okay, fair enough. It's a bit unlikely that the Time Lords would let one of their own roam free on a world where he was likely to impregnate the indigenous population, but it kind of explains the Doctor's affinity for Earth and his quintessential Englishness (and occasional Scottishness). But if the frequency of his trips to particular planets is a criterion on which to base the Doctor's origins, he might as well be half-Dalek. Anyway, if suddenly owning up to being half-human means he is able to get off with his assistants, surely he'd have done it years ago. All those glimpses of Jo Grant's knickers should have prompted him to mention it; and when Nyssa was parading around Terminus in her underwear, why didn't he just say 'Have I ever told you about my mother?' There are a couple of good reasons why he ought to have let Peri in on it. We could go on and on . . .

HEMAL: Uniquely, a black Time Lord, seen in comic strip form in Marvel's 1995 *Doctor Who Yearbook*. Presumably, this was an attempt at Political Correctness; what it actually says is that there are black people on Gallifrey, but that few of them distinguish themselves by becoming renegades, being elected on to the High Council, etc, else we'd have seen them before. Nice try, though.

HERTS PLASTIC MOULDERS DALEK: Uninspired-looking mid-sixties Dalek toy, although this didn't deter US publishers Avon Books from sticking a photo of a couple of them on the front of the American paperback edition of *Doctor Who in an Exciting Adventure with the Daleks*; even with the addition of sparkler weapons, they hardly looked formidable enough to provide adventure, exciting or otherwise. The toy was produced in both black and grey. However, as a collector's item, it has become overshadowed by its companion piece . . .

HERTS PLASTIC MOULDERS MECHANOID: For many years this elusive item was a virtual holy grail to collectors of vintage *Doctor Who* memorabilia. Its appeal lay not only in its scarcity, but also in the fact that it was the only decently produced sixties toy spin-off not to be based on the ubiquitous Daleks (Cherilea manufactured a range of smaller and inferior

Mechanoids in a choice of colours). To own a Herts Mechanoid guaranteed a place of high honour within the *Who* collectors' hierarchy – that is, until the fateful day when a vanload of the little buggers turned up on Preston Market, thus ending the Mechanoids' only real stab at notoriety.

'HE'S BACK ... AND IT'S ABOUT TIME': Tag line used to promote the Paul McGann movie, although *Radio Times* rather missed the point by quoting it as 'He's back ... and about time too.' We might suggest that 'He's back ... but what the hell's it about?' could have been as appropriate. Or how about 'He's back ... but not for long!'?

HEXACHROMITE: A gas fatal to reptilian life forms. Phew, lucky there were plentiful supplies of the stuff on Sea Base 4 when the Silurians and Sea Devils arrived aboard.

HIDING IN PLAIN SIGHT: Pantomime precaution often taken by the Doctor and company to avoid detection by monstrous forces. This is especially characteristic of Seasons Sixteen and Seventeen, but can be seen as far back as 'The Dalek Invasion of Earth', in which a Dalek glides past the 'concealed' Doctor with its eyestalk pointed straight into his face but fails to notice.

HINES, FRASER: Cornerstone Communications' second and best attempt at spelling Frazer Hines's name on their trading cards.

HODDLE, GLEN: One rather optimistic punter actually placed a bet on 'Dr Who' replacing Terry

Venables as England manager. We don't know the odds, but it turned out to be a waste of money. Though if Glen had declined . . . Much better if the guy had gone to William Hill; there, he could have got 14m/1 on a UFO piloted by Elvis Presley crash-landing on the head of the Doctor's one-time (or is that two-time?) enemy, the Loch Ness Monster. Surely that's worth a quid of anyone's money?

HOLMES, SHERLOCK: One of the great characters of popular fiction, and one with much in common with the Doctor: they are both eccentric intellectuals without any obvious interest in women. Yet it seems to be impossible for the same person to portray both successfully. So far, two actors of not inconsiderable talent have attempted it, both getting only halfway towards accomplishment. As Sherlock Holmes, Peter Cushing vies with the likes of Basil Rathbone and Jeremy Brett for the title 'definitive', but his dotty old grandfather interpretation of the movie Dr Who rarely if ever receives favourable comparisons with the TV incarnations. Tom Baker may have won international acclaim and huge ratings as the fourth Doctor, but his appearance as Holmes in BBC's *The Hound of the Baskervilles* even provoked a derogatory comment in the corporation's own handbook (it might be worth mentioning that, while visiting Victorian London, the fourth Doctor exchanged floppy hat and long scarf for deerstalker and Inverness cape, but then again, as the authentic Holmes of Conan Doyle's stories never dressed like that, it might not). Fans of the two characters have something in common too. Holmesians can ponder over such continuity problems as why, in 'The Final Problem', Doctor Watson claimed never to have heard of Professor Moriarty, when he'd encountered him in *The Valley of Fear* (a novel written after but set prior to 'The Final Problem'). Likewise, *Doctor Who* fans have many hundreds of similar gaffes to worry about. Some readers might expect us to mention the New Adventure *All-Consuming Fire* here, however Holmes was instrumental in enabling the Doctor to overcome a much earlier and greater spin-off challenge; that's right, he appeared in the *Doctor Who* Trump Card Game!

'HOPPITY-HOP, BOPPITY-BOP, WHO'S NEXT FOR THE CHOP?': Endearing rhyme that accompanied a playground execution game of the Meeps when they debuted in the best ever *Doctor Who* comic strip, 'Doctor Who and the Star Beast' (*Doctor Who Weekly* issues 19–26). These once-lovable alien furballs developed a spacefaring civilisation despite spending most of their time joining hands and dancing around in circles ('Hop, skip, jump and sing, four jolly Meeps all in a ring'). Alas, Black Star radiation changed their dispositions, and they had to be hunted down and slaughtered by genetically engineered Wrarth warriors. Their Most-High, Beep, escaped and crash-landed on Earth, where he found shelter with two kids called Fudge and Sharon, until the latter called him a 'furry little cheeky' and he knew she had to go. Sharon was rescued by the Doctor and went on to become his first ever black companion, as he whisked her away from her home town of, erm, Blackcastle. Fudge, meanwhile, returned in the 1996 *Doctor Who Yearbook*, only to become Beep's target once again. This full-colour strip confirmed what the *Classic Comics* reprint of 'The Star Beast' had recently postulated: that the Most-High was white. Whoever coloured him blue in the American version deserved a good Grundian blood-nog.

TEN NOTABLE MARVEL COMIC STRIPS

1: 'Doctor Who and the Iron Legion' (*Doctor Who Weekly* issues 1–8). The Doctor lands in an old *Star Trek* plot where Rome never fell, and finds himself battling the Ecto-Slime in a gladiatorial arena.

2: 'A Cold Day in Hell' (*Doctor Who Magazine* issues 130–3). When Marvel produced their first McCoy strip, they had no idea what his costume would be like. To avoid the issue, they spirited him off to a freezing planet and decked him out in Troughton's fur coat. When McCoy wore that very item in 'Time and the Rani', a continuity triumph was claimed. However, this was offset by the inclusion in the strip of Frobisher, bemoaning the recent loss of Peri. Indeed, 'A Cold Day in Hell' finally ruined any claims to canonicity that the comics had ever had. It's also worth mentioning the debut of a new companion, Olla the heat vampire; barely, though, as she died the following month.

3: 'Business as Usual' (*Doctor Who Weekly* issues 40–3). The best of those back-up strips they used to run, in which the Doctor would be seen in a head-and-shoulders shot introducing an adventure of some old friends or foes. This one pitted industrial spy Max Fischer against the Autons who, rather unusually, won and presumably went on to conquer the world. The strip was reprinted in *Doctor Who Magazine* issue 84, although Tom Baker's face was replaced by Sylvester McCoy's to cause confusion.

4: 'Doctor Who and the Iron Legion' (*Doctor Who Summer Special 1980*). The Doctor lands in an old *Tomorrow People* plot where Rome never fell, and finds himself up against General Ironicus and the youthful but dangerous Emperor Adolphus, with only the ageing robot Vesuvius beside him.

5: 'The World Shapers' (*Doctor Who Magazine* issues 127–9). Grant Morrison takes gross liberties with continuity, but so far he hasn't been contradicted. The Voord evolve into the Cybermen, Jamie returns as an old man but dies, Planet 14 is revealed to be Marinus, and the Doctor tells the Cyber-Controller there to remember his and Jamie's auras as they'll meet again (aah, fanboy glow).

6: 'Evening's Empire' (*Doctor Who Magazine* issues 181– erm . . .). Acclaimed by readers as the best strip in ages, at which point Marvel promptly lost the final instalment and, shrugging its shoulders, went on to the next tale. The denouement was revealed at last in a special edition of *Classic Comics*, long after the event.

7: 'Doctor Who and the Iron Legion' (*Marvel Premiere* (USA) issues 57–8). The Doctor lands in an old *Superman* plot where Rome never fell, and struggles to keep the despicable Magog from taking over his TARDIS.

8: 'Ship of Fools' (*Doctor Who Weekly* issues 23–4). Another back-up strip, this one a sequel to an earlier effort and featuring the return of Kroton, the Cyberman with a human soul (no relation to the walking egg boxes that conquered the Gonds). Drifting through space, he is picked up by the *Flying Dutchman II* and helps its crew out of a timewarp, only to watch as they all age and die. Kroton is left alone in the universe again. Aww, shame.

9: 'Doctor Who and the Iron Legion' (*Doctor Who Summer Special 1985*). The Doctor lands in a forerunner of a Missing Adventure plot where Rome never fell, and is caught between the evil Malevilus and the brutal Bestarius.

10: *Age of Chaos* (1994). Intended as a four-part mini-series, this sixth Doctor tale – written by Colin Baker himself – had to be repackaged as a one-shot special when the UK arm of Marvel collapsed in on itself. It features the Doctor's visit to Krontep and a cameo appearance by a future Peri, firmly scotching the rumour that she'd taken Yrcanos to New York and set him up as an all-in wrestler.

HOSTILE ACTION DISPLACEMENT SYSTEM (HADS): See CONVENIENTLY FORGOTTEN TARDIS FUNCTIONS.

***HYPERION III*, LAXITY OF THE SECURITY ARRANGEMENTS ABOARD:** Why do all the cabin doors on this luxury space liner seem to have the same key? No wonder the security officer turned into a murdering psychopath!

I

IDENTITIES OF THE ALIEN DELEGATES IN 'MISSION TO THE UNKNOWN': The script refers to them as Gearon, Trantis, Sentreal, Malpha, Beaus, Celation and an unnamed Black Dalek. However, the names that were seen on screen were, reportedly, Malpha, Desmir, Stifka, Hgbuj, Pteron, Leemon and Dbremen (not to mention that Dalek again). This apparent discrepancy has long been a subject for fierce debate.

'INCIDENTALLY, A HAPPY CHRISTMAS TO ALL OF YOU AT HOME': The last line of 'The Feast of Steven' and the single sentence that brought *Doctor Who*'s credibility crashing down around William Hartnell's ears. How can we trust the character again, if even he knows he's an actor in a TV programme? Where possible, fans have tried to forget that this travesty occurred. It's ignored in the novelisation, and audio copies of the (thankfully missing) episode have until recently had the offending line removed. Our theory, however, is that the Doctor, remembering his recent adventure at the space museum, was simply mindful of the fact that citizens of the future could have been sitting at home and watching his escapades on their time/space visualisers.

'INDEFINABLE MAGIC': A term coined by fans who cannot for the life of them explain why they watch a tacky, cheap kids' show. 'Well, it has that indefinable magic, dunnit?'

INHERITORS OF TIME, DOCTOR WHO AND THE: In the mid-eighties, American writer John Ostrander, known primarily for his comic book work, acquired the stage rights to *Doctor Who*. In order not to contradict the established and subsequent TV continuity, he devised a completely new incarnation of the Time Lord. In his version, set in the far-distant future, the Doctor is long since dead (relatively speaking, of course); requiring his services yet again and having curtailed the longevity of his second incarnation, the Time Lords, feeling they owe him half a life, resurrect the Doctor to save the universe or whatever. Little else is known about the plot of this play – by us at least, and we can't be bothered checking – although we think the Inheritors of Time referred to in the title were actually the people of Earth who acquire the Time Lords' mantle. Roger Müeller, an American, was signed up to portray the Doctor and Lee Ditkowsky brought in to provide special effects for this half-million dollar production. The play was all set to premiere at The Pickwick Theatre, Park Ridge, Chicago when one of the major backers pulled out. It never opened, much to the relief of UK fans at the time. For one thing, they wouldn't have been able to see it. But more importantly, they knew that Americans, not having a clue about what makes for decent *Doctor Who*, would have made a complete arse of it.

'INSIDE NICOLA BRYANT': Intriguing article promised on the cover of *Doctor Who Magazine* issue 166 but not delivered within.

ION BONDER: Tubular implement possessed by Nyssa of Traken, which was discarded when it became strangely water-logged in 'Castrovalva'. Nyssa made up for her loss by borrowing the Doctor's sonic screwdriver in the following story, and was so impressed that she spent the whole of 'Kinda' in her bedroom with the device. Unfortunately, the Terileptils destroyed the screwdriver in 'The Visitation' and Nyssa was forced back into her room to build something bigger and better. She was still missing her little friend in 'Black Orchid' when Tegan ordered a 'screwdriver' and Nyssa, misunderstanding, requested the same. What this all means, we're not sure.

'IS THERE A DOCTOR IN THE HORSE?': Provisional episode title that was never used during 'The Myth Makers', but should have been.

IS THERE ANY POINT IN BRINGING BACK THE SILURIANS IF THEY'RE MADE TO LOOK DIFFERENT?: It's cool to change the way the Cybermen look: they're machines, fashions change, they looked crap in 'The Tenth Planet' . . . In rare instances, it's even acceptable to change the appearance of biological species. Take *Star Trek*'s Klingons, for instance, which were originally made to look alienesque by the application of boot polish to their faces; after that, even a cornish pasty stuck on the head looks better. There was, however, no excuse for changing the Silurians in 'Warriors of the Deep'. As far as rubber-suited monsters go, their debut look was entirely acceptable. Just because *Teenage Mutant Ninja Turtles* was popular when they returned, it was no reason to bestow them with shells. But as they did, why not claim these ones were another off-shoot of the race, and not add insult to injury by pretending that one of them was acquainted with the Doctor from the previous skirmish?

I WAS A DOCTOR WHO MONSTER: Interesting as the anecdotes from Sonny Caldinez, Stephen Thorne, et al are, the most noteworthy aspect of this nostalgic tribute video has to be the stunning recreations of studio recordings featuring actors who look nothing like the companions they're supposed to represent. Even Sophie Aldred manages to look not much like Ace.

J

J: The forbidden letter of the Dalek alphabet, at least according to 'The Dalek Dictionary', a section of that wonderful mid-sixties publication, *The Dalek Pocketbook and Space Travellers Guide*. We had it in mind to try and disprove this by citing an example from the series in which a Dalek is heard to exclaim a word with 'J' in it. However, as this would have meant scrutinising hours of tedious Dalek episodes, we'll let Terry Nation's claim go unchallenged for now. 'The Dalek Dictionary' provides many fascinating facts about life on Skaro and gives a basic grounding in Dalekese; however, it shamefully omits the word 'Exterminate'.

TEN QUITE INTERESTING THINGS IN 'THE DALEK DICTIONARY'.

1: *Alvega.* A planet populated by fighting plants under the command of a root. The Daleks invaded Alvega but got twatted by the vegetation.

2: *Arkellis.* A rare Skarosian flower that will only take root in metal. Hey, that sounds like one hard plant species — maybe they should have taken on the Alvegans.

3: *Baz.* A Dalek screw. No, not that kind of screw — minds like sewers, you lot.

4: *Cellulise.* A miniaturisation process that renders things

91

so tiny as to be virtually invisible, even under a micro-scope. Yep, that's small all right.

5: *Flagee.* The Dalek word that means to punish. With extermination, presumably.

6: *Galkor.* Translates as 'Follow me, I am your guide'. We don't recall a Dalek ever uttering the word 'galkor'. 'Exterminate' perhaps, but never 'galkor'.

7: *J*: Actually, it is possible for Daleks to say the letter; it's just that it's their equivalent of swearing, for which they would no doubt be flageed.

8: *Nesd.* Means 'I warn you to beware!' Quickly followed by 'Exterminate! Exterminate! Exterminate!' no doubt.

9: *Pentorrokon.* A five-headed monster, which, the dictionary reveals, is 'now, happily, almost extinct'. Good thing too – it puts the wind up us just reading about it.

10: *Zyquivilly.* Farewell.

<hr>

JAIL: Ultimate destination of the other-dimensional sorceress Morgaine, who was left in UNIT's custody by the Doctor. What are they going to do, draw a chalk circle around Holloway or something?

JEANS: Non-regulation clothing daringly worn by a Cyberman in the Death Zone, as presumably it was a bit nippy there, and anyway it didn't want to stain its silver pants whilst lying behind a wall in the hope that a Doctor would walk by. A precedent for cold-weather clothing was set by the original Mondan Cybermen, who fancied themselves in fur-hooded anoraks. This was a particularly frightening scene for fans, as it demonstrated how easily the soulless monsters could penetrate an SF convention.

JENKINS, GARETH: Before we start, we ought to mention that Jim first fixed it for someone to meet the Doctor in the mid-seventies when Tom Baker materialised in the studio in costume and in character.

Now there's a bit of info you won't find in *Doctor Who – The Seventies*. Anyway, before people start thinking this is a proper factual book, let's get on ... When eight-year-old Gareth Jenkins wrote in requesting to meet the Doctor and have a gander at the TARDIS, he got more than he bargained for and ended up starring in a *Doctor Who* adventure of his own, alongside Colin Baker and Janet Fielding as Tegan. And it must be said that, of the *Doctor Who* adventures broadcast in 1985 featuring Sontarans, the return of a former companion and two 'Doctors', 'A Fix with Sontarans' is far and away the superior. Oh yes, it is 'A Fix with Sontarans' not 'In a Fix with Sontarans' – that would just be silly. More recently, along similar lines, David Petter (aged eleven) wrote in to *Surprise, Surprise* and ended up getting a full-size 'Remembrance' Dalek worth several grand! Hmm, 'Dear Cilla ... '

JUNIOR DOCTOR WHO: Short-lived series of books that undertook to rewrite the Target novelisations for a younger audience. This idea was based on the mistaken belief that the books were selling to adults in the first place. Those of us who found we had to step back three paces for the gargantuan print in *Planet of Giants* to resolve itself into letters knew the unfortunate truth.

K

KAMELION: Humanoid animatronic model left over from the seventies SF robot boom. Someone had the bright idea of using it in 'The King's Demons', but forgot to check if it worked first. It didn't, and was thus consigned to the back room of the TARDIS, refusing to show any of its faces even for 'The Five Doctors'. Kamelion could make himself resemble any person in the thoughts of his companions, which must have been useful on those long lonely nights. However, the first time he left the ship, he was brutally murdered by the Doctor. This was perhaps for the best, as an examination of Kamelion's history reveals the possible existence of a curse of Poltergeist proportions. Both Terence Dudley and Peter Grimwade, who scripted the robot companion's appearances, have sadly passed away. So too have Kamelion's human alter-ego, Gerald Flood, and Dallas Adams, who played his 'Howard Foster' form for most of 'Planet of Fire'. To say nothing of Kamelion's software designer, Mike Power, who was killed shortly after the decision was taken to include the robot in the series. Eric Pringle should thank his lucky stars that a Kamelion sequence was edited out of 'The Awakening' and Missing Adventure scribe Craig Hinton should start worrying.

KEMBEL: A planet featured in 'The Daleks' Master Plan', a story which was co-written by Terry Nation and

Denis Spooner. A similarly named planet turned up in an episode of *Fireball XL5*, also written by Denis Spooner. Just a coincidence, or could this perhaps have been an early BBC/ITV cross-over?

KENNEDY, JOHN F: Political figure whose assassination shocked the world by delaying the first ever episode of *Doctor Who*. It is said that everyone can remember where they were when news broke of Kennedy's death. That's probably because half of them were sitting in front of the telly and thinking 'Bloody hell, they're running late, when's *Doctor Who* coming on?'

KILROY: A bit-part character in 'Warriors' Gate' played by Mike Mungarvan. He was one of Rorvik's crew and, when their ship exploded, Kilroy was everywhere.

'KINDA': Christopher Bailey's innovative script for this Season Nineteen story incorporated themes of Buddhism and Christianity into the well-trodden *Doctor Who* framework of a colonial intrusion upon an alien culture, creating a narrative of considerable semiotic thickness that was given an in-depth analysis in John Tulloch and Manuel Alvarado's seminal academic work, *Doctor Who – The Unfolding Text*. On screen, 'Kinda' showcased an impressive guest cast, including Nerys Hughes, Richard Todd, and Simon Rouse (who provided a hauntingly realistic portrayal of a true psychotic personality). It also introduced the Mara, a unique and terrifying creature that lurked within the dark corners of the mind and which deservedly became the first recurring *Doctor Who* monster for over eight years. Sadly, the appearance of a massive great wobbling rubber snake at the end renders this whole production worthless.

KING DICK: Did you know that Julian Glover, who played Richard the Lionheart in 'The Crusade', reprised the role years later in a TV movie version of *Ivanhoe*, also directed by Douglas Camfield? Okay, we know this entry isn't rude or amusing, as implied by its heading, but we wanted to draw your attention to this interesting snippet of information.

KINGDOM, SARA: Despite being dead, she was a major protagonist in the pilot script for Terry Nation's proposed Dalek TV series for America, and she starred in her own comic strip in *The Dalek Outer Space Book* ('The two crooks who tried to rob Sara Kingdom were unaware that she possessed the strength of ten men'). But was she a proper companion or what? Well, if tripping about in the TARDIS for a few episodes of one story before dying horribly is the only criterion, then yes. But she was hardly a series regular, was she? This, we feel, brings into question the legitimacy of her 'official' status: surely there ought to be a minimum requirement for achieving this honour, even if it's only appearing in two stories before dying horribly! Hmm, that Katarina, was she a proper companion or what?

KKLAK!: As near as can be represented, this is the sound made by the snapping of a pterodactyl's jaws.

'K9, K9, DOO DOO DOO DE-DOO DE-DOO, K9': Memorable lyrics to the theme tune of the 1981 spin-off story *K9 and Company*, available on the Solid Gold Label, SGR 117.

KRANG: The name of our favourite ever fanzine, and also that taken by a Cyberman in 'The Tenth Planet', which goes some way towards explaining why they never admitted to having names again. As an awe-inspiring, threatening appellation, Krang has to rank up there with Tarpok, Bok and Yartek, Leader of the Alien Voord.

K2: Professor Kettlewell's robot, newly possessed of self-awareness and still growing when we met it. It was cruelly destroyed by UNIT, even though it only played with Action Men and lusted after the Doctor's companion. Which adolescent male of the time did less?

KY: Garrick Hagon's character in 'The Mutants', and not to be confused with the commercially available lubricant jelly of the same name.

L

LARYNGITIS: Virus contracted by the Doctor's mechanical mutt in 'Destiny of the Daleks'. Normally, this would have stood out as a ridiculous idea, however of the three recurring characters who were recast for the Season Seventeen opener, K9 was given the best excuse.

LAZAR DISEASE: Nasty space illness, one of the symptoms of which is for the sufferers to remove their clothes and replace them with filthy rags.

LIMITED EDITION 'GHOSTS OF N-SPACE' TAPE WITH LUMINOUS COVER: So what if calling it a limited edition is a ploy to get people to buy it 'before it sells out', and in truth it's only limited to the number of copies the BBC expect to sell anyway (and then some)? If you hold it really close to the bulb and then switch off the light dead quick, it glows like mad for ages. In fact, it's guaranteed to provide hours of fun and enjoyment – which is more than you can say for the tapes within.

LIVERPOOL: The first Doctor visited this North West city during a Christmas break from thwarting the Daleks' Master Plan. Surprisingly, no one nicked the TARDIS while he was there.

LLANGOLLEN, *DOCTOR WHO* EXHIBITION AT:
An extensive collection of items comparable with those at Longleat and the late-lamented Blackpool. On our one visit, however, we noticed that certain exhibits were rather eccentrically labelled, leading us to the conclusion that the people staging it weren't as clued up on *Doctor Who* as they might have been. This could result in some unscrupulous fan taking advantage of the situation by volunteering their services then systematically substituting clever replicas for genuine items, thus acquiring an authentic collection of props and costumes. For example, a simple garden gnome could be switched with the Malus, and a rubber plant with a photo cut out of *Razzle* pasted on to the top would be a convincing Vervoid. Visitors would notice the difference, but assume that the originals weren't available.*

* If you decide to try this super wheeze, please remember who gave you the idea and bung us a couple of Plasmatons in the post.

LOADED: Laddish magazine, based on babes, beer and football, which described *Doctor Who* as 'the TV equivalent of anal warts', and its fans as 'anorak-clad wankers'. Fair enough, but see *STAR TREK* FANS.

LOCATION SPOTTING: The perfect answer to those people who say you should get a life and get out more. Why not take a trip to Aldbourne and thrill to the exciting locations at which 'The Dæmons' was made? Or Portmeirion, home to 'The Masque of Mandragora' (a bit of a problem there: you have to avoid the mad *Prisoner* fans). The only trouble is, you soon run out of vaguely interesting spots and end up with the gravel pits. 'Ah yes, this is where the Doctor was first seen in "Tomb". No, come to think of it, it was that identical bit there. Or was that where they filmed "The Hand of Fear"? No, just a minute, this is where they did all 52 episodes of *Blake's 7*.' On second thoughts, if you want to see the locale at which your favourite story was filmed, go and buy the video. Chances are, it'll look a lot more interesting on that.

LOCH NESS MONSTER: Hmm, bit of a dilemma here. There appear to be two candidates for the role of Scotland's favourite tourist attraction, and we feel there's room in the *Doctor Who* universe for only one true 'Nessie'. So let us properly consider the suitability of the applicants. Firstly, the Skarasen: large reptilian animal, closely resembling the creature described in many recorded sightings; once featured in a novel entitled *Doctor Who and the Loch Ness Monster*; lives in Loch Ness. Now the Borad from 'Timelash': little bloke with an ugly mug who may have visited the area. Your votes please.

LONDON (FACTUAL): English capital, enlivened by the siting of several *Doctor Who* landmarks within its boundaries. The sight of Westminster Bridge or Saint Paul's Cathedral cannot fail to stir memories of classic stories. Likewise, the underground system fairly echoes to the imaginary roars of Yeti, although Marble Arch station looks little like it did in 'The Trial of a Time Lord'. For a time, an added attraction could be found in Tooley Street's 'permanent' *Doctor Who* Exhibition – the third in the country, and the first to showcase the Kandyman and a simply magnificent Plasmaton. Despite its proximity to the city centre, the exhibition lost out because of a frankly inadequate public transport network. The only way to reach it was to travel via Mars in a space shuttle, adding greatly to the time and cost of the journey.

LONDON (FICTIONAL): The unlikely target of 99 per cent of invasions, which was lucky for Earth as UNIT happened to have a big base there with a good scientific adviser. Had any malevolent ETs hit upon the idea of attacking, say, Dublin, we might now be living under the yoke of alien oppression.

LONGLEAT: Stately home and grounds in Wiltshire, famous for its lions. A popular UK tourist attraction, it is ideally placed to avoid all major public transport routes. We had to travel down with our DWAS Local Group in a Rent-a-Wreck van, holding the door shut all the while lest it fly open and catapult us into the middle lane of the motorway. An eight-hour round trip was justified, however, by the discovery that Longleat boasts the biggest maze in Europe. The signs claim that you will be stuck in there for sixty to ninety minutes, but one of us spent two hours trying to find the centre whilst the other climbed over a gate and then couldn't find his way back out again. Oh yes, there's a permanent *Doctor Who* Exhibition there too, and sometimes they change the displays a bit.

LOPEZ: Not Polly's surname (the character played by Anneke Wills, that is; for all we know, there could be hundreds of people called Polly Lopez out there), despite the claims of those who have somehow managed to misinterpret the dialogue in 'The Faceless Ones'. Fortunately, those years of tedious research into *Doctor Who*'s origins were made worthwhile by the discovery that this popular sixties dolly-bird's surname was in fact Wright. Yes, highly imaginative of the *Doctor Who* team, that, to give her the same name as one of her predecessors, especially as they'd only used four at that point (see KINGDOM, SARA to see why we don't count her). It was quite lucky, then, that the writers forgot to use it anyway. Her first name, on the other hand, must surely have been inspired by 'Polly put the kettle on', as she shared the tea-making proclivities of this nursery rhyme's title character. As a bit of posh totty whose presence was mainly decorative, Polly . . . erm, Wright was not a prototype for the liberated females who succeeded her; however, her beverage-preparing antics did prove useful against the Cybermen.

LOST STORIES: From unfilmed Hartnell scripts like 'The Masters of Luxor' through to plans for Season Twenty-seven (along the lines of dumping Ace on Gallifrey in favour of a safe-cracking replacement), many intended stories have become casualties of everything from budgetary restrictions to the recurrent cancellation of the series. Trouble is, the dropped stories always sound more interesting than those actually made, what with singing Space Whales and suchlike. Surely between them, the BBC costume, make-up and visual effects departments could have run off 96,000 Gallifreyan Killer Cats? And logistics aside, a story by acclaimed SF author Christopher Priest had to be better than at least one of those by people who weren't acclaimed SF authors, yet sadly his 'Sealed Orders' remained that way. Target provided what ought to have been an ideal opportunity to disprove the notion about lost stories being better when they novelised some of the scripts from the cancelled Season Twenty-Three, and they turned out to be not much cop. But then to improve upon 'The Trial of a Time Lord' they didn't have to be. In order to put paid to this myth once and for all, we recommend that some brave publisher bring out 'The Dark Dimension' as a script book.

NINE LOST *DOCTOR WHO* STORIES, PLUS ONE EMBARRASSING MISTAKE MADE BY A GULLIBLE FANZINE WITH THE INITIALS DWB

1: 'The Hidden Planet'.
2: 'The Rosemariners'.
3: 'Erinella'.
4: 'Valley of the Lost'.
5: 'Hex'.
6: 'Paradise Five'.
7: 'The Dogs of Darkness'.
8: 'Alixion'.
9: 'Guardians of Prophecy'.
10: 'The Opera of Doom'.

M

MAGISTER, THE REVEREND: Not-so-cunning pseudonym of the original Master which, along with a Clark Kent-type pair of glasses, allowed him to completely conceal himself in Devil's End. Okay, so 'Magister' is Latin for 'Master', but what he apparently failed to notice is that it's only two letters different from the English translation, rendering it less than deceptive to anyone but Jo.

MAGS: Native of Vulpana with great legs. Fortunately, when she transformed into a slavering, fanged, crazed werewolf kind of thing, as Vulpanans are wont to do, her legs didn't get all hairy and gross. We were quite pleased about that.

MAJOR DISASTERS: The Doctor has saved our world many times over, but that must be cold comfort to the descendants of the *Marie Celeste* crew. Doubtless they were appalled to discover that, in luring the Daleks on to that famous ship, the Doctor caused the deaths of all on board. Not content with that act of mayhem, he persuaded Nero to torch Rome, started the Great Fire of London – twice – and stood by whilst the Cybermen wiped out the dinosaurs. What an absolute bastard.

***MAKING OF DOCTOR WHO, THE* (PICCOLO**

EDITION): For years, fans' comprehensive *Doctor Who* reference libraries consisted entirely of this book. For even more years, this excellent publication had the unique distinction of featuring on its cover the first (pre-diamond) Pertwee logo – even *The Seventies* went straight for the diamond version. But *Making of*'s pre-eminence has been cruelly usurped by a plethora of publications purporting to feature the 'McGann logo'.

MANCHESTER: North West city and footballing capital of the universe. Not to be confused with the entirely dissimilar city of the same name that featured in the Missing Adventure *Goth Opera*. We should know.

'MARY HAD A LITTLE LAMB': Nursery rhyme which, when reversed by the Master in 'The Dæmons', became a potent spell. Pip and Jane Baker took the idea one step further when, in their novelisation of 'Time and the Rani', they revealed that Tetraps spoke in reverse English. Unlike Barry Letts, they felt the need to give us not only an explanation of this, but also a sample translation. Skcollob fo daol a tahw (what a load of rubbish).

MASTER, THE: He's nutty as squirrel shit, he always loses, and he's so rubbish he even played second fiddle to the Rani (another alleged super-villain whose major talent, however, seems to be her Bonnie Langford impersonation). So why is he reputed to be the Doctor's greatest enemy?

MASTERPLAN 'Q': Way back in 1971, Nestlés – who didn't pronounce the accent on the 'e' in those days in case xenophobic brits boycotted their products in favour of more English-sounding confectionary –

produced a *Doctor Who* chocolate bar with Pertwee's distinctive features carved into it. Even more interesting, though, were the wrappers, on the backs of which – spread over fifteen thrilling instalments – was a third Doctor story in 'cartoon' form: *Doctor Who Fights Masterplan 'Q'*. This early Missing Adventure has received little coverage elsewhere, hence the following detailed synopsis: Exploring the primeval planet Quorus, the Doctor and Jo are forced into hiding by the arrival of a giant dinosaur. They are even more surprised, however, to see their old foe the Master, clearly up to no good. From their hiding place, they watch as the Master produces a control device and tames the huge beast. He leaves Quorus in his TARDIS and the Doctor and Jo follow. The Doctor is horrified to see that the Master's course will take him to Earth. The evil Time Lord makes his way to McMaster Electronics on the Yorkshire Moors, where he puts the next phase of Masterplan 'Q' into operation. He hands a sack of giant eggs to his lab assistant, Jenkins, and orders him to place one inside the reactor. It hatches to produce a miniature version of the dinosaur on Quorus. It doesn't remain tiny for long, though: the Master bombards it with ultra-violet light and it grows to astronomic proportions. With the assistance of the police and armed forces, the Doctor is finally able to pick up the Master's trail. Amidst the rubble of the now-wrecked McMaster factory, he discovers the cracked eggshell and realises what his enemy's game is. He is met with incredulity when he attempts to explain his theories, but all disbelief vanishes when an Air Force officer reports a flattened trail leading to the top-secret weapons research centre at Darisdale. Setting off in Bessie, the Doctor explains to Jo that Darisdale houses Britain's first transporter beam. It was designed to transport detachments of men and machines to any location on Earth, and it can easily do the same for a gigantic alien reptile. However, an officious Major refuses the Doctor and his companion entry to Darisdale, but as they leave, the Master watches from inside the barricade. As the Doctor and Jo drive back across the moorland, they hear a terrifying thumping sound. The dinosaur is hunting them down. As the beast approaches, the Doctor presses a switch on Bessie's dashboard. The monster is engulfed by thick exhaust fumes and lumbers away. Back at Darisdale, the Master and the treacherous Major put the final part of the plan into operation. They transport the dinosaur to Leicester Square and the Master broadcasts a sinister message: 'At any given time, I can transport my pet anywhere in the British Isles. You have 24 hours to surrender all power to me!' Meanwhile, disguised as a despatch rider, the Doctor gains access to the facility and awaits his chance. Seeing that the Master controls his creature with an ultra-sonic sound box, he ponders the consequences of interfering with its frequency. He blows on his own ultra-sonic whistle, and the dinosaur breaks free from the Master's control . . . Bugger! Has anyone got wrapper number fifteen, so we can find out how it ends?

McGANN, JOE: Actor who didn't play the eighth Doctor, despite what you may have read in the *Daily Mirror*.

McGANN, PAUL: Great, a bloody Liverpool supporter as the Doctor! Sheesh, to some of us Manchester-based fans that's virtually on a par with casting Robbie Fowler in the lead. Paul is obviously a popular choice elsewhere, though – Renault even seem to have named a car after him!

TEN ACTORS WHOSE NAMES HAVE BEEN BANDIED ABOUT IN CONNECTION WITH THE LEAD ROLE IN *DOCTOR WHO* OVER THE YEARS, WHETHER THEY WERE REALLY UP FOR IT OR NOT (INCLUDING A COUPLE THAT MARVEL ONLY SEEMED TO MENTION BECAUSE THERE WAS NOTHING ELSE TO PUT IN 'GALLIFREY GUARDIAN' THAT MONTH)

1: Cyril Cusack.
2: Ron Moody.
3: Jim Dale.
4: Richard Griffiths.
5: Brian Blessed.
6: Tony Robinson.
7: Joanna Lumley.
8: David McCallum.
9: Eddie Izzard.
10: David Burton.

Oh, and while we're at it . . .

TEN MORE ACTORS WHOSE NAMES HAVE BEEN BANDIED ABOUT etc

11: Donald Sutherland.
12: Sylvester Stallone.
13: Tim Curry.
14: David Hasslehoff.
15: Eric Idle.
16: Alan Rickman.
17: John Cleese.
18: Dudley Moore.
19: Sting.
20: Richard O'Brien.

And Simon Callow too . . . and Leslie French, and . . .
Oh sod it!

MEGALON: Scientist who, following an accident with one of his experiments, became the Borad. He must have decided that Megalon was just too obvious a name for a megalomaniac.

'MEN OUT THERE, YOUNG MEN, ARE DYING FOR IT': Broadbrush statement included in an Atrian recruitment video, as seen in the opening moments of 'The Armageddon Factor'. The speaker was, of course, referring to the speculative young men's love of their home planet. However, if you consider his utterance out of context and think about it hard, you'll see that it could equally apply to the act of sexual intercourse, which is amusing.

MERCHANDISE COLLECTING: When you examine this hobby, it does seem rather pointless and silly, especially the purchasing of non-practical items that can't be watched, read, etc. The only reason for it seems to be oneupmanship: when a *Doctor Who* collector invites his fellow collectors up to his room and says 'Let me show you my latest acquisition, an extremely rare Plastoid Menoptra/Venom Grub badge', he actually means 'I've got one of these and you haven't. Na na na-na na'. Big deal, a Cowan deGroot Clockwork Dalek is hardly a status symbol in the same league as, say, a Jaguar XJ 220, is it? Ultimately, it's a waste of money too. How many *Doctor Who* fans will have children interested in inheriting a pair of wooden William Hartnell jigsaws and a Dalek skittle set? Indeed, how many *Doctor Who* fans will have children? So when, after a lifetime spent hoarding Bendy Daleks and Davison Easter eggs, the *Who* collector snuffs it, all that will happen is that the relatives will pack his junk into bin bags and dump it at the local Oxfam shop, where it will be purchased for a generation of children who no longer remember *Doctor Who* and so will destroy it at the first opportunity. It brings to mind the old adage as seen in the back window of many a Vauxhall Cavalier: 'If you can't smoke it, screw it, or eat it, throw it away' (unless you can drink it, that is).

METEBELIS 3: There aren't many things in life more pathetic than commenting on a spellchecker's off-target suggestions, but the computer's helpful recommendation that we replace this planet with the word 'meatballs' did raise a little smile.

MIDNIGHT OPENINGS: Attending the one in London remained within the bounds of acceptability, due to the personal appearance by director Geoffrey Sax. However, elsewhere in the country, queueing up outside HMV in the middle of the night to purchase a copy of 'The US Telemovie with the Pertwee Logo', when it would be widely available the following morning and on telly less than a week later, is nothing short of tragic. Admittedly, we were at the Manchester one, but purely to observe this cultural phenomenon first-hand. Okay, so one of us bought the video, but only because under the circumstances it became convenient to do so, and furthermore it was for a friend.

MINOTAURS: Over the years, *Doctor Who* has featured a load of old bull, and never more so than when it has ripped off (sorry, paid homage to) the legendary inhabitant of the Athenian labyrinth. Only a few years before he became Darth Vader, the ultimate screen villain of all time, Dave Prowse was given the opportunity to create an equally memorable protagonist for TV. Alas, somebody stuck an unconvincing bull's head on him, rammed glycerine up its nostrils to make it look fierce, and told him to caper around a cheap labyrinth set until he walked into a wall and fell over. Rather more convincing was the costume used several years earlier in 'The Mind Robber', although the knowledge that it's worn by Mr Sparrow from the brewery in *EastEnders* diminishes its impact. After 'The Time Monster', you'd have thought the series would have learnt its lesson but, lo and behold, later that very decade the same bit of classical mythology was plundered again. The Nimon (a partial anagram of 'Minotaur', clever eh?) camped their way through Season Seventeen's final story with woolly heads, silly skirts and obviously plastic horns. They never returned.

MIRE BEAST: See MONSTERS THAT LOOK A BIT RUDE.

MIRROR SCENE: For years, we heard about the magical scene – sadly missing from the archives – in which a newly regenerated second Doctor looked into a mirror and saw his former self reflected. Now, thanks to recently unearthed cine footage, we can view this thrilling slice of yesteryear in its full glory, as Patrick Troughton reaches down and picks up . . . a photograph of William Hartnell in a mirror frame! Thus are long-cherished illusions shattered. Morris Barry must have suffered a similar disappointment when, shortly after he was interviewed on camera about 'The Tomb of the Cybermen', the story was rediscovered and his comments about its fantastic special effects were cruelly juxtaposed against the rather sad reality.

MISSING CONSONANTS: It has come to our attention that some fans who obviously have no lives at all like to play at taking consonants out of the names of *Doctor Who* stories to form something different. Allegedly amusing examples include 'The Tree

Doctors', 'The Greatest Sow in the Galaxy', and of course the ever popular 'Colon in Space'. No doubt you can think up your own, if you're so inclined.

MISSING ADVENTURES: Misleading generic title for a series of original novels featuring Doctors one to six. From what are they missing exactly? What's that, you say? 'From the shelves of discerning readers'? Now, that's a bit unkind. Obviously, these stories are absent from the TV series since, apart from featuring the Doctor and the TARDIS, most have about as much in common with TV *Doctor Who* as they do with *Pets Win Prizes*; certainly no one ever caught the clap on the telly version (*Doctor Who*, that is – we can't speak for *Pets Win Prizes*). And then there's *The Ghosts of N-Space*; blimey, don't say BBC Radio have gone and lost it already. No matter, we know where there's a couple of unwanted copies going spare.

MOGARIANS: The one sure way of picking out these aliens from a crowd is described in Pip and Jane Baker's novelisation of their own 'Terror of the Vervoids'. Apparently, their names all end in a vowel and contain a 'z'. It is perhaps fortunate that the Doctor wasn't travelling with Zoe when he encountered them, as that would have only caused needless complications.

MONK, THE MEDDLING: Amoral, yet otherwise likable, Time Lord who had no qualms about altering history for his personal gain. It is likely, therefore, that he was responsible for introducing potatoes into Britain centuries earlier than they would otherwise have arrived, presumably envisaging a potential goldmine in a chain of Medieval chip shops. As the natural flow of time has apparently been restored, it must be assumed that, following his encounter with the Sontaran Linx, the Doctor removed all offending anachronistic spuds and left Walter Raleigh to claim the full credit. See also POTATOES.

MOVIE, THE BLOCKBUSTING, MEGA-GROSS-ING *DOCTOR WHO*: No really, there was going to be one and John Cleese was going to be the Doctor. Or was it Dudley Moore? No, definitely Donald Sutherland. But anyway, Caroline Munro was going to be in it, because she's married to one of the producers (from Coast to Coast . . . No, Green Light. Erm, Daltenreys?), and she was absolutely, positively cast as the companion . . . or villain. The script was written by Johnny Byrne, or someone else, and it was going to be called *Doctor Who – The Movie*. Until they changed it to *Doctor Who – Last of the Time Lords*. One thing is certain: it would have been brilliant. But then again . . . Another movie that didn't get made was *Doctor Who Meets Scratchman*. This one didn't star Tom Baker as the Doctor, nor did it feature Vincent Price as the villainous hellspawn of the title. Twiggy didn't play the companion, either.

MYRKA: Less than terrifying pet of the Silurians and Sea Devils, which cavorted its way into Sea Base 4 during 'Warriors of the Deep' lacking only a comedy 'quack' sound effect. It says something about the production team's own opinion of its design that they chose the two blokes who played the pantomime horse in *Rentaghost* to bring life to this uncomfortably similar creation. Presumably, John Perrie and William Asquith's experience in childrens' farce helped them to remain straight-faced during such hilarious moments as Ingrid Pitt's karate kick and the bendy polystyrene door. Actually, there is a school of thought which says that monsters like this are really very clever. In a universe of infinite wonders, there's no reason to assume that the dangerous ones will fulfil our preconceptions of them. The Zygons and the Terileptils may appear as we expect alien conquerors to appear, but the Myrka, the Zarbi and the Taran beast all have as legitimate a claim on realism. After all, the Doctor once met a purple horse with yellow spots at the Third Intergalactic Peace Conference; he said so. So, next time fans of *Star Trek* and *Babylon 5* are deriding your beloved programme for its cheapness, just try that argument and see if it doesn't shut their lying mouths for all time (warning: it might not).

N

NAME DROPPING: The Doctor has always been a little guilty of this, particularly in his third incarnation. Since he possesses a time machine, there's no point in doubting he's actually met the people he claims, but who is he trying to impress? Those familiar with the workings of the TARDIS will presumably find hearing names like Napoleon, Churchill and Alexander the Great mentioned a touch mundane. Anyone else listening to the Doctor spouting on about having tea with Ghengis Khan or someone will just think he's a nutter.

NEBROX: Character from the *Blake's 7* episode. 'Assassin' played by Richard Hurndall, who spent most of the episode practically naked but for a big nappy. Watching this performance, John Nathan-Turner claims to have been greatly reminded of William Hartnell.

NEMESIS STATUE: It used to be that the Doctor was a simple wanderer in space and time who quietly slipped away from his people in a broken-down old TARDIS. Nowadays we have to believe that, on his way out, he stockpiled all the Time Lords' greatest weapons in case he needed them to commit genocide against the Daleks, the Cybermen, etc. In the course of one such plan, he sealed the Nemesis statue into a comet (bearing an uncanny resemblance to a jaffa cake) and sent it into an orbit that returned it to Earth every 25 years. Each time it passed, it caused disasters: in 1913 it was the Eve of the Great War, 1938 was the Eve of World War II, and 1963 was the assassination of President Kennedy (not, repeat not, the first Dalek invasion, from which the Doctor and Ace had just come). Sadly, no one could think of a disaster in 1888, which would have continued this trend. But let's get this straight: the Doctor unleashes a weapon that causes the two biggest wars in history and the murder of a respected political figure, then brings the Cybermen to Earth to kill yet more people, all so that they'll reassemble the Nemesis statue and trigger it against themselves. Forgive us our scepticism, but why didn't he just use it when he had it?

NESTENES: A collective race who have been colonising worlds for 1,000,000,000 years, though presumably only those with thriving plastics industries.

NEW ADVENTURES – HOW TO GET ONE ACCEPTED: First, you need to give it a title. Normally, if you were writing a proper *Doctor Who* serial for television the sensible thing would be to call it something reflecting the content, like *Invasion of the Evil Alien Monsters* or *Terror of the Master's Shrinking Thing*. However, with a New Adventure it's a better idea to give it a name that's irrelevant but snappy and perhaps a little controversial too (they'll like that). Something like *Arse* ought to do it. Alternatively, you couldn't go far wrong with something epic and biblical, like *Deuteronomy* or *St Paul's Letters to the Corinthians II*. It is essential that you make some reference to cyberspace. When the New Adventures began, this was quite a new concept and only novels that harped on about it at great length were commissioned, the editors believing it would be the next big thing. Sadly, Virgin still seem intent on appealing to the techno-nerd readership, although cyberspace has now joined the ranks of out-moded SF cliches like bug-eyed green men from Mars with ray guns (they use the Ice Warriors too). So think on, and make sure you include a cyberspace/computer-based subplot. It might be tricky to insert it into your fifteenth-century historical, but in the long run it'll be worth the effort. Finally, it's crucial to include liberal doses of sex and violence, particularly if it's the Doctor's companions indulging in both and preferably at the same time. Good luck!

NEWSPAPER COMIC STRIPS: Whilst serving his time as editor of *Doctor Who Magazine*, John Freeman attempted to get a seventh-Doctor newspaper strip off the ground. Judging by the varying styles of the prototype examples, it seems John wasn't sure whether the papers would prefer *Doctor Who* to be a competitor to Garth or to Andy Capp. As it turned out, they didn't care much either way. Maybe if he'd brought back Peri and done it in the style of Jane?

NINE, OBLIQUE ONE TWO, OBLIQUE FOUR FOUR: Reference number used by Turlough in 'Planet of Fire', and also attributed to Halley's Comet in 'Attack of the Cybermen'. An astonishing coincidence, that.

NUDITY, BLATANT: We saw sadly little of this on screen. However, the writers of non-visible media have always been quick to have the main characters flop 'em out, perhaps missing the point that it's a bit of a waste of time for them. It's hardly surprising that the New and Missing Adventures are the main offenders, given their obsession with the sort of activities for which clothes are an impediment. The very first New Adventure began with Ace in the buff, and she has been followed by a succession of others – not least amongst them Peri, whose state of undress went unnoticed by the Doctor when a freak indoor flash flood washed her out of the shower and into the TARDIS console room at his feet! *Happy Endings* celebrated the fiftieth New Adventure with a nudie outdoor romp involving Benny, Jason Kane, Ace again, an Ice Lord and the Doctor himself. However, 'The Paradise of Death' had already beaten Virgin to the punch where this latter was concerned. Fortunately, neither story expounded upon the specifics of Time Lord anatomy, and various fan theories about the Doctor's number/lack of reproductive organs remain unconfirmed. Presumably, no one dared to look down. See also *GIRL ILLUSTRATED*.

NUMBERING OF *DOCTOR WHO* STORIES: It used to be simple. No one ever disputed that 'The Stones of Blood' was the 100th story, even if most people thought the proposed birthday cake scene was a stupid idea. But only a year later, things went to pot. Should the unfinished 'Shada' be considered 109, or should it be skipped over? Was 'Slipback' canonical? And how many distinct stories comprised 'The Trial of a Time Lord': one, because that's how it was credited; three, because that's how many production codes it had; or four, because that's how the writing teams were assigned? Does the BBC announcement that 'Dragonfire' was the 150th mean that they're counting 'Trial' as four, or that they've recognised 'Shada', 'Slipback' and *K9 and Company*? If *The Discontinuity Guide* lists 'Dimensions in Time' as being 160th, though chronologically 110th, why shouldn't we number the equally valid 'A Fix with Sontarans' and 'Doctor Eyes'? And what about the third-Doctor radio plays and the New Adventures? It's all getting a bit tricky.

NUNTON EXPERIMENTAL COMPLEX: Bob Baker and Dave Martin's setting for much of the action in 'The Hand of Fear'; not to be confused with the Nuton Complex that appeared in their earlier work 'The Claws of Axos', and which was clearly not the same place at all.

NYSSA'S SKIRT: Item of clothing removed on screen by actress Sarah Sutton as a parting gesture to fans during her final regular appearance, in 'Terminus'. This partial strip was condemned as scandalous and sexist by some sections of fandom (the ones who don't get out much). On the contrary, it was a lovely thought, and ought to have set a precedent for future female companions – well, the good-looking ones anyway.

———————◆———————

TEN PEOPLE WHO REVEALED THEIR UNDERWEAR IN *DOCTOR WHO*

1: Nyssa. Heeding fans' complaints about her always wearing trousers, she considerately flashed those gams. (Interestingly enough that's how she started out: in 'The Keeper of Traken' part three the Doctor helpfully lifted up her skirt when that gust of wind failed to do the job. It's true, really; go and have a look.)

2: Turlough. Although following Nyssa's lead, he saluted a different group of viewers by getting off his keks for his final story, 'Planet of Fire'.

3: Peri. After wearing next to nothing throughout her tenure, her leaving gesture was to put on some clothes for 'The Trial of a Time Lord'.

4: Zoe. Her knickers were spotted on screen almost as often as in rehearsal (see EYEPATCH JOKE, THE).

5: Isobel Watkins. She obviously thought 'The Invasion' was a panty flashing competition with Zoe (although actress Sally Faulkner didn't bother wearing any in *Confessions of a Driving Instructor*). Jamie decided against joining in, even going to the trouble of having weights sewn into the hem of his kilt, so we never found out if he was a real Scotsman. Fortunately.

6: Leela. Being rather modest she made sure that when she had to parade round in her undies in 'Talons' it was those all-covering Victorian ones. A pity then (for her) that they got all wet and completely transparent later in the story. She must have learnt her lesson, for in 'The Invasion of Time' she took the precaution of going swimming fully clothed, although to make up for it, she did flash her knicks in part six.

7: Barbara. Ian accidentally debagged her whilst holding her on to the roof of the Mechanoid city in 'The Chase'.

8: Jo. She flashed her underwear several times – she even managed to display two different pairs in 'The Time Monster' when they changed from white to yellow between episodes (given that this was such a scary adventure, this could just prove that the wardrobe department had an astounding eye for detail) – but Katy Manning can't be too bothered, what with her *Girl Illustrated* spread and all.

9: The co-pilot in 'The Horns of Nimon', whose dramatic death scene in part two is tragically undermined by the appearance of a huge split in his pants.

10: And finally, who can forget Ian's open dressing gown in 'The Edge of Destruction'? Well, we certainly can.

O

ODDBALL STORIES: Term coined in the late eighties to refer to those episodes in which mad cleaning robots and walking liquorice allsorts proliferated. Many fans were incensed by this sub-genre, often hurling that most nonsensical of accusations, 'It's not real *Doctor Who*!' They bemoaned the inclusion of fantastical elements and demanded a return to the basics of men in rubber suits and lots of corridors (the 'archetypal adventure', as in 'the same plot as last week'). It's worth noting that the 'oddball' tag can only be applied to latterday stories. Earlier escapades with Keystone Kops, giant board games, and fairy tales come to life, escape criticism because, having been made in the sixties, they must be 'real'. See also FAN REACTION.

OPEN FACE: Anatomically repulsive and presumably unhygenic disfigurement attributed to the fifth Doctor by Terrance Dicks in many Target novelisations.

ORGANISED SIGNINGS AT SF SHOPS: Fantastic events that are well worth visiting – that is, if you're the retailer who's organising them. Anyone else should stay away, unless they're keen to boost said retailer's sales and pay a hefty admission fee for the privilege. Even the most pathetic convention provides better value per guest than these blatant displays of profiteering.

OUT-TAKES: Over the years, much footage has left the BBC Archives, in one way or another, that wasn't included in broadcast episodes. Some of this provides intriguing glimpses into the production of *Doctor Who*, and the studio rushes of 'Death to the Daleks' certainly do that – for about a second until you realise how dull they are. If you don't want to find your eyes drifting to the comparatively interesting stretch of wallpaper behind the TV, you're better off seeking out some of the filmed occasions on which things have gone wrong. One or two of these are actually funny, which by *Red Dwarf*'s standards is enough to fill two over-priced BBC Video releases. Until *Doctor Who* follows suit, however, fans have to search through old episodes of Noel Edmonds shows to find, amongst other clips, the demolition of a lych-gate by a horse in 'The Awakening' and an amusing fall by McCoy in 'Silver Nemesis' (far more so, as it happens, than those that were left in 'Time and the Rani'). Harder to find are the genuinely dangerous accidents that befell Sophie Aldred in 'Battlefield' (see EYEPATCH JOKE, THE) and the hapless War Machine operator who abandoned his smoking machine in a bit of a hurry. Also, to the best of our knowledge, the clip from 'Planet of Fire' in which a German nudist (the same one who 'rescued' Nicola Bryant – see EYEPATCH JOKE, THE again) walked through the shot has not been broadcast. A third type of out-take is more readily available, in a few cases at least. Scenes or lines cut from transmitted episodes have been edited back into some stories as an excuse to jack up the price of the video release. For the most part, these give a fascinating insight into the reasons why the scenes were cut in the first place. It's nice to see what they actually made of 'Shada', though, and the 'Silver

Nemesis' video is indispensable as they seem to have put back the most important parts of the plot. Now, if only they'd taken out the rest of it instead . . .

OWEN, DAVE: Intelligent, witty bloke with tons of sex appeal and an amazing talent for hilarious limericks. What a guy! Dave writes the book reviews for *Doctor Who Magazine*.

P

PANDY, ANDY: Popular children's character, clearly beloved of Sarah Jane Smith as she dressed in his image for 'The Hand of Fear'.

PARALLEL UNIVERSES: Favourite and cost-effective idea of all science-fiction TV series. It precludes the need for guest stars as the regulars get to dress up in leather gear, moustaches and of course eyepatches, and pretend to be their own evil counterparts. What a pity *Doctor Who* made only one excursion into parallel realms; it would have been interesting to see a sixth Doctor adventure of this type, and a lot of fun trying to spot which Doctor was the evil version. Admittedly, Peri in leather has a certain appeal too.

PATTERN BOOK, THE DOCTOR WHO: Who says people won't buy any old crap just because it's got the *Doctor Who* logo on it? Oh all right, it's plain jealousy: would that we could devise a book as funny as this one. Indeed, the cover price is justified by the full-page photo of Action Men decked out as Doctors one to six (come on you older fans, own up, how many of you got your mums to knit a *Doctor Who* outfit for your Action Man?). There's no denying that this book is extremely useful if you ever feel inclined to 'knit a nasty' or sew together 'Adric's Anorak'; as an added bonus the accompanying photographs show how to turn your room into an authentic replica of the TARDIS interior simply by sticking paper plates on the walls.

PEEING (OVER A SHELF): Uncharacteristic bodily function carried out by the Doctor in the book *Delta and the Bannerman* (sic).

PERIGOSTO STICK: A device of unknown specifications, near which you should not allow a Venusian Shanghorn to be. This is, apparently, very funny.

PERI'S TITS™: Twin companions to the fifth and sixth Doctors. The fact that there was a woman attached to them was incidental, at least to some directors. If the script said 'Peri trips up', then camera directions would read 'Zoom straight down cleavage'. John Nathan-Turner claimed that the presence of the scantily clad Peri was drawing male viewers to *Doctor Who* in droves. It also drew a number of press photographers to a topless beach in Lanzarote, in the vain hope that the show's new star would flop 'em out.

PERIVALE: See BARBARAVILLE.

'PICKED UP BY THE GUARDOLIERS': Unpleasant fate that apparently awaited Herbert George Wells in 'Timelash'.

'PICKLED IN TIME, LIKE GHERKINS IN A JAR': The opening line, pre-titles, of 'Dimensions in Time', really setting the scene for what was to follow. We still don't know what the Rani was on about, any more than we know who 'that terrible woman' was, why an imaginary line like the Greenwich Meridian could be important to her plans, or how a so-called

128

twenty-year time loop could encompass four decades.

PINBALL MACHINE: Released by Bally to celebrate (well, make money from) *Doctor Who*'s thirtieth anniversary. It boasted a plot more complicated than that of 'Ghost Light': the Master and Davros were using a time expander to catapult all seven Doctors into the sun and the only way you could rescue them was by knocking a few balls around a playing surface. Rescue them? You'd have done well to recognise them from those drawings! The promotional video boasted that the machine would be 'as timeless and enduring as Doctor Who himself'. Well, as the series had been four years dead at that time, it was probably right. A little easier to play was the *Doctor Who* fruit machine, although this disappointed by having little to do with the programme at all. From its name, we had expected the reels to include Alzarian marsh fruits, those melon things on Segonax, 'Revenge' Cybermen, etc.

PINK TERILEPTIL: Imitation monster that visited Thoros Beta during the Doctor's stay.

PIRATE VIDEOS – HOW TO OBTAIN THEM: You could do worse than go into a reputable video stockist, approach the assistant and say: 'Excuse me my good man [if it's a bloke], do you perchance have a copy of the widescreen edition of *Devil-Ship Pirates* starring Christopher Lee? Or perhaps some equally thrilling swashbuckler with Errol Flynn?' As far as pirated copies of *Doctor Who* episodes are concerned, with the rise of satellite TV and the regularity of BBC Video releases, it seems they've had their day. It's a bit sad, really. It was so much more exciting in the old days: twenty people huddled around a telly at a local group meeting, transfixed by flickering images of indistinct, barely audible figures lurching through even more snow than is usually found at the South Pole, convinced that they were watching a first-generation copy of 'The Tenth Planet' part one. However, thanks to the BBC's insistence on butchering the McGann movie by removing the so-called violent bits, fans have had a brief opportunity to recapture the feeling of those heady days of yesteryear by getting together to watch grainy converted copies of the American broadcast, with the action scenes thankfully intact (and you wondered where those two kids disappeared to at the start?). Thanks again, Beeb, for allowing that fleeting nostalgic experience.

POINTLESS BUTCHERY: Why do BBC Video persist in cutting the final scenes from most Hartnell adventures? Someone must think we're all too thick to cope with the concept of a cliffhanger leading into the next story, even if that story is in the same boxed set!

POINTLESS REPETITION: Never mind staircases, the one thing that most consistently scotches Dalek plans for universal conquest is their penchant for repeating themselves. It's no use floating up the stairs after your mortal enemy if you're only going to chant the word 'Exterminate' eight times until he escapes. Likewise, Romana is given seven orders to remain still in 'Destiny of the Daleks', despite having shown no signs of movement. Amongst other examples, *The Ultimate Adventure* stands out for its Daleks' somewhat less dramatic, but similarly over-stated, intention to keep the Doctor alive ('alive, alive, alive!'). We don't mean to imply, though, that this is merely a Dalek perogative; just watch 'Attack of the Cybermen' part one, the cliffhanger to which resembles nothing more than a line from 'Bohemian Rhapsody'. Also, less tactful writers might be tempted to point out that the plot of 'Silver Nemesis' was a pointless repetition of that of 'Remembrance of the Daleks'.

'POLLY ACCOMPANIED BEN THROUGHOUT HER STAY IN THE TARDIS': An entire chapter from John Nathan-Turner's book *Doctor Who – The Companions*. This was exhaustive coverage in comparison to the section devoted to Jo Grant: 'Katy now lives in Australia'. The piece on Zoe, though, wins hands-down as a profound exercise in minimalist writing. It simply reads: ''. In John's defence, he did refrain from likening Tegan to an East End slapper. No, he waited until his memoirs feature in *Doctor Who Magazine* issue 237 for that. By the way, have you noticed that the illustrations in John's book make practically everyone look boss-eyed?

POSTER AND POSTCARD BOOKS: Basing our findings on information received from a mate who works in a specialist science-fiction bookshop, we can exclusively reveal that, in fact, fans won't buy any old crap with the *Doctor Who* logo on it!

POTATOES: By a clever trick of time travel and poor research, Sarah Jane was able to peel these in the twelfth century, before they were actually brought into the country. At least, so the novelisation of 'The Time Warrior' claims, although it is a common misconception amongst fans that the mistake appears in the televised version as well. A cursory viewing shows that this is not the case; presumably, the rumour was put about by someone who felt that *Doctor Who* didn't already contain enough gaffes to poke fun at.

In fact, it wasn't until the mid-eighties that the series enjoyed its first unambiguous association with the popular root vegetables, as Golden Wonder gave away miniature *Doctor Who* comics with their crisps. The strips used were taken from Colin Baker's run in the Marvel magazine, but with half the story missing in each case; a bit like some BBC videos we could mention.* They now fetch sums of up to 20p at conventions.

Although, come to think of it, 'The Time Warrior' is one of those videos. Perhaps someone hacked out the line, 'Hmmm, thanks for these lovely chips, Sarah,' without our knowledge.

PROTECT AND SURVIVE: As a public service in 1976, 'The Hand of Fear' educated viewers about sensible precautions to take in the event of a massive nuclear strike. Its advice, as relevant now as then, was to find shelter behind a handy jeep. Alas, the explosion from which the Doctor and company were hiding did not occur, so we can only speculate as to whether the idea would have proved more effective than the recommended tin of white paint.

PUDSEY BEAR: This animated ursine mascot of the *Children in Need* appeal made an unwelcome guest appearance in 'The Five Doctors' as transmitted in southern regions of the UK. How we laughed, up here in Manchester (although it didn't quite make up for our transmitter failure during *K9 and Company*). Still, if you've not got one of the dozen or so video releases of this story by now, you obviously weren't that bothered.

PSEUDO-HISTORICAL: One of those terms that only exists within the confines of written studies of *Doctor Who*, like 'oddball story' and 'classic Holmesian double-act'. This label is applied to any adventure set in Earth's past that features science-fiction elements (in

132

contrast to the 'pure/straight historical', which seems an odd description of 'The Romans' and 'The Gun-fighters'). The word seems to imply that the story is pretending to be a straight historical, which isn't the case when you think about the overt alien presences in 'The Visitation' and 'The Mark of the Rani'. By the same logic, 'The Enemy of the World' is presumably the programme's only stab at 'pseudo SF'.

'PSEUD'S CORNER': A column in *Private Eye* that printed the following extract from an *In-Vision* article by Alec Charles:

> A source is only as good as its provenance. Postmodern writers are constantly pained and inspired by the anxieties and uncertainties of influence: fears of mis-quotation, pretension and plagiarism fuel the nightmares of literati as their forebears were once haunted by the charge of heresy, treachery and homosexuality. The history of the production, performance and reception of the *Doctor Who* story 'Kinda', closely addresses this paradox of literature's indebtedness to a canon which purports to prize originality as its last best virtue.

We can't understand why *Private Eye* saw fit to include it: it all seems perfectly reasonable to us – whatever it means.

PYRAMID ON MARS, A: If reports in the press are to be believed (and we're not talking *Sunday Sport* here), Glasgow school children studying NASA images of the red planet have spotted a pyramidal structure on its surface. There you have it, another stunning real-life prediction from *Doctor Who*.

Q

QUARKS: Following in the grand tradition of the Daleks and the Cybermen, these creatures won the hearts of a nation with their fierce determination, breath-taking destructive capabilities and realistic tottering gait. They debuted in the classic 1968 serial 'The Dominators' (named after the story's secondary protagonists to preserve the impact of the metallic marauders' revelation in the closing moments of part one), excellently realised by actors John Hicks, Gary Smith and Freddie Wilson. Credit must also go to Sheila Grant (presumably not the *Brookside* character), who provided the galactic gladiators with their distinctive shrill, some might say creepily incongruous, voices. So impressive were the Quarks, in fact, that they were chosen for an early return to the programme, to help round off the very season which they had successfully launched. It is regrettable that only one Quark actually appeared in 'The War Games', but we are fortunate that the BBC were able to procure the acting talents of Freddie Wilson a second time, maintaining that vital link of continuity in a way that didn't seem to matter with lesser adversaries such as Davros, the Master and Omega. Sadly, as *Doctor Who* was hurled from the world of sixties monochrome and into the hi-tech rainbow hues of the Pertwee era, it was decided that the Quarks were not ideally suited to this new world of colour. With great reluctance, the BBC passed the responsibility for their awesome automatons to an eager *TV Comic*. It is gratifying to note, however, that the Quarks, along with their similarly inspired contemporaries the Krotons, were the only monsters of the Troughton era considered important enough to be left untouched by the archives purge of the seventies – a fitting act of recognition, we feel, for these fine creations.

QUARRIES: Terran geological features, which freakishly resemble most alien planets. The Doctor and his friends spent many a happy half-hour being pursued around grey gravel pits, until the hi-tech of the eighties was brought to bear and they were able to run around multi-coloured gravel pits instead. 'The Hand of Fear' offered a marvellous piece of self-awareness for the show as, emerging from the TARDIS into a quarry on present-day Earth, Sarah Jane mistook it for another world. Alas, she went on to completely ignore a warning siren, was buried under a ton of rubble, and might well have died had Eldrad not given her a hand.

QUESTION MARKS: Towards the end of his fourth incarnation, the Doctor began to display these symbols to prove what an enigmatic kind of guy he was. For many years, they remained understated on the shirt collars of successive costumes. Then, it was decreed that Sylvester McCoy's character should be very enigmatic indeed – far more so than any of his predecessors – which meant that lots more proof of his mysterious nature was required. Thus we got the question-mark umbrella, the question-mark calling card, the question-mark jumper and more than likely the question-mark shark repellent had the Doctor only been called upon to use it (although the biggest question mark of this period was, of course, the one hanging over the show's future). Thankfully, Paul McGann reversed this trend, thus sparing us its only logical progression: an eighth Doctor in the Riddler's costume.

QUIZ BOOK OF DINOSAURS, THE DOCTOR WHO: Just one in a series of informative fifth Doctor paperbacks published by Magnet (the others, if you really need to know, covering Science, Space and Magic). Author Michael Holt delivers many fascinating facts about these popular prehistoric monsters, but neglects to mention the Cybermen's involvement in their untimely demise. The fifth Doctor himself seems to be suffering from a touch of post-regenerative amnesia; when questioned by Nyssa about the Loch Ness Monster, he speculates that it may be a surviving Plesiosaur. See LOCH NESS MONSTER for a couple of other possibilities.

R

RADIO: *Doctor Who* has made several excursions into the world of the wireless, most of them with actual people from the telly and everything. It can be argued that radio is the perfect medium for the series, being exempt from rubber monsters, wobbly walls and the sixth Doctor's costume. But can the audio-only productions be counted as official entries in the canon, apocryphal tales, or about as authentic as the New Adventures? Read the next list and we'll tell you.

TEN AUDIO *DOCTOR WHO* ADVENTURES AND THEIR RESPECTIVE CLAIMS TO CANONICITY

1: *Whatever Happened to Susan Foreman?* Modern-day reporters interview people involved in the story of 'time-travel girl Susan Foreman' for a programme re-examining a thirty-year-old scandal. Interviewees include Susan, Ian Chesterton, Barbara Wright, Jo Jones (née Grant) and Claire Rayner (who advised Susan that her grandfather had no right to take her out of full-time education). Susan reckons the Doctor dumped her because he didn't want some girl hanging about calling him 'Grandfather' while he got off with a stream of bimbos. The writer did his homework to an extent, but unforgivably had Temmosus survive 'The Daleks'. Also, no TV people were featured. Claiming that Carole Ann Ford was asked cuts no ice with us.
Canonicity Rating: 1

2: 'The Paradise of Death'. Full marks for reuniting Jon Pertwee, Lis Sladen and Nick Courtney, although the Doctor also acquires an irritating git called Jeremy (expertly played by television's Dennis the Menace, Richard Pearce). Sarah Jane meets the Brigadier for the first time again, and for this alone, we've marked it down.
Canonicity Rating: 7

3: 'The Ghosts of N-Space'. The Doctor goes into N-Space (but not the proper one) and meets some ghosts (though he's since claimed not to believe in them). The Brigadier's great uncle Mario speaks with the most convincing Italian accent since Chico Marx.
Canonicity Rating: 6

4: *Exploration Earth:* 'The Time Machine'. A Radio 4 schools programme, starring Tom Baker and Elisabeth Sladen. It was intended to educate children about the origins of Earth, but might have left them with the confusing impression that a Lord of Chaos was hanging about for most of the process. Meggron of the Carrion race, voiced by John Westbrook, isn't one of the greatest *Doctor Who* villains. He only really threatens to give the Doctor and Sarah headaches with his undeniable shouting ability. Dunno where it fits, but there's nothing to suggest that the Doctor couldn't have had this adventure.
Canonicity Rating: 8

5: 'Genesis of the Daleks'. The BBC must have really liked bits of this story, as they kept repeating edited highlights. They also released some on LP, with fresh narration by Tom Baker to close the gaps. Years later, a similar format was used for audio copies of missing episodes, but in the days before most people had video recorders this was all we could get and it was appreciated. Sadly, despite mentions of time rings in the dialogue, the Doctor claims to have arrived on Skaro in the TARDIS.
Canonicity Rating: 8

6: *Doctor Who and the Pescatons*. This one's unique: a new adventure on LP, starring Tom Baker and the seemingly ubiquitous Lis Sladen. We're not convinced that you can see the surface of Pesca with a telescope, but that was only in the novelisation, so we'll let it pass.
Canonicity Rating: 9

7: 'Slipback'. Eric Saward attempts to do *Hitch-Hiker's* and fails. He never forgets it's actually *Doctor Who* though, so there's plenty of reassuring lusting after Peri and running up and down corridors. All right, so it contradicts 'Terminus', but who's to say how many detonators the Big Bang needed anyway? The sixth Doctor getting rat-arsed is also strangely in keeping.
Canonicity Rating: 9

8: Panasonic Batteries Advert. A little short, but certainly the finest seventh-Doctor Cyberman story. It starred Sylvester McCoy, Sophie Aldred and David Banks, and used the proper theme music instead of that spangly affair usually associated with McCoy. The advert doesn't really contradict anything seen on television: the implication that Cybermen use cheap batteries can be seen as a natural progression of the series' continual weakening of the race. It is implied that the TARDIS might run on Panasonic batteries, but at least it's more plausible than that Eye of Harmony stuff in the telemovie.
Canonicity Rating: 10

9: Audio Visuals. Excellent 'unofficial' audio adventures of the Doctor, produced by Bill Baggs before he could afford to buy video gear and, latterly, by Gary Russell.
Canonicity Rating: 7, but we reserve the right to lower this to 0 in the event of the TV Doctor reaching his thirteenth life without being played by Nick Briggs. Also worth mentioning are *The Stranger* audios, starring Colin Baker as a character who isn't a bit like the Doctor at all, no sir. A series called 'Time Gash', featuring Sylvester McCoy and Sophie Aldred, was also advertised, but we've never seen it. Good thing too; it couldn't possibly be as interesting as its name suggests.

10: 'Professor Prune and the Time Trousers'. *Who*-inspired radio serial that ran through the 1969 series of *I'm Sorry, I'll Read That Again*. Professor Prune (Graeme Garden) and his Cockney niece Trixie (Jo Kendall) pursue the evil Fetish (John Cleese) through time and space in dimensionally transcendental pants. Also starring Bill Oddie, Tim Brooke-Taylor and David Hatch.
Canonicity Rating: sadly, 0.

***RADIO TIMES DOCTOR WHO TENTH ANNIVER-
SARY SPECIAL:*** A *Radio Times Special* published to
celebrate the tenth anniversary of *Doctor Who*, if you
hadn't already guessed. It is now a highly sought after
collectors' item, and deservedly so. By and large it is
excellent, with just one or two things that only the most
finnicky pedant could split hairs over. So here we go:
for one thing the Hartnell stories were identified by the
first episode titles, which if nothing else at least meant
they got 'An Unearthly Child' correct. Then there are
those specially done photos of *Doctor Who* cast members from the first ten years. A great idea, but unfortunately this was the seventies, so the likes of Michael
Craze and Peter Purves who looked reasonably sensible
whilst in the series, now appeared with long girly hair
and flares. Some of the former cast members fared
better than others for their photocalls: Wendy Padbury
was allowed to wear her normal clothes while alluding
to the intellectual Zoe by being surrounded by lots of
computer tape, yet poor Carole Ann Ford was forced to
get dressed up in mangy flea-ridden furs (as like as not
this was a reference to the first ever story, although that
doesn't really explain the plastic dinosaurs in the background). Worst of all, however, was the Nick Courtney
shot, which shattered so many illusions by betraying
the fact (due to the total absence of any facial fungus)
that the Brigadier's moustache was a fake! No anniversary *Doctor Who* publication would be complete without
some Dalek features – which is a shame but there you go
– and this one was topped off with detailed instructions
for building what would turn out to slightly resemble one
of the metal meanies from Skaro, and a brand new Dalek
adventure by Terry Nation – another account of their
origins we shouldn't wonder. If anyone's ever bothered
to read it let us know. Ten years later, *Radio Times*
published a *Doctor Who Twentieth Anniversary Special*,

142

which of course gave them the opportunity to produce a magazine twice as good as the one described above. But they didn't.

RANDOMISER: Whilst fleeing from the Black Guardian, the Doctor fitted this device to his TARDIS, ensuring that nobody – not even he – knew where he was going to land next. In this respect, it did him something of a disservice, taking him first to Skaro and then to twentieth-century Earth. Had the Guardian been so bothered about finding him, the most casual check of his usual haunts would have done the trick.

RASSILON: Materialistic founder of the Time Lords; included amongst his many possessions were the Ring of Rassilon, the Sash of Rassilon, the Rod of Rassilon, the Coronet of Rassilon, the Key of Rassilon, the Scrolls of Rassilon, the Game of Rassilon, the baseball cap of Rassilon, and the Hand of Omega . . . Hand of Omega? Hang on, that can't be right! How did Omega wangle that one, then?

RASTON WARRIOR ROBOT: Silver spandex-clad gymnast that threatened the Cybermen with its sinister ballet dancing and disturbing bulge.

RAT, GIANT: Wouldn't you know it, an otherwise faultless tale marred by the appearance of an unconvincing, yet cuddly, rodent. Still, let's be positive about this: at least the sewer scenes in 'The Talons of Weng-Chiang' allowed us a glimpse of Leela in wet Victorian underwear. Incidentally, giant rats were unusually common in seventies telefantasy shows; well, one turned up in *The New Avengers*, although we suspect this was mainly a device to enable the use of the really clever title 'Gnaws' – sounds like *Jaws*, geddit? Hilarious.

REAL POLICE BOXES: Ho hum, talk about per-petuating the myth. The recently refurbished police box in Glasgow's Buchanon Street actually has a plaque that mentions *Doctor Who*. Unfortunately, it goes for that old chestnut about the BBC using a prop left over from *Dixon of Dock Green* for the original TARDIS. The other plaque crediting Terry Nation as the creator of *Doctor Who* must have fallen off. We did learn, however, that up until the end of the sixties, Glasgow police boxes were painted red, instead of the familiar blue. That's a bit interesting, isn't it? Maybe they saw the first colour *Doctor Who* stories and realised their mistake.

RED TELEPHONE BOXES: The appearance of one of these (with the word 'police' written on it) as the TARDIS on the cover of the Japanese edition of *Doctor Who and the Daleks* leads us to suspect that the pub-lishers, Hayakawa, were not supplied with much in the way of reference material. Likewise, the inclusion of a green TARDIS in the US comic-book adaptation of the film *Dr Who and the Daleks* leads us to suspect that Dell weren't provided with much in the way of colour reference material. And while we're at it, the time-travelling phone box in *Bill and Ted's Excellent Adventure* makes us pretty certain that the cheeky sods ripped off *Doctor Who*.

REFUSIANS, SPIRIDONIANS AND VISIANS: Given the cost of latex, races of invisible aliens always come in handy on a no-budget SF show like *Doctor Who*.

REGENERATION: The origins of this exceptional Time Lord ability have never been properly explored within the confines of the television series. It's not really surprising, though, that precious minutes of plot development haven't been wasted simply to explain whether this capacity is a genetically engineered augmentation or just part and parcel of the Gallifreyan evolutionary process, as to do so would have cut down on crucial scenes involving corridors and running. It is enough to know that regeneration is a wonderful concept, without which *Doctor Who* would doubtless have been a very short-lived affair (wonder if James Bond is a closet Time Lord?). But astonishing capability or not, it's a bit much that the third Doctor's arm regenerated complete with tattoo!

REJUVENATION: Ridiculous theory, albeit one put forward unilaterally by *Doctor Who Monthly*, that the second Doctor was simply a younger version of the first and not a fully-fledged regenerated Doctor in his own right (Pat Troughton was a dead ringer for the young Bill Hartnell then, was he?). This theory was subsequently blown out of the water by dialogue in both 'Mawdryn Undead' and 'Time and the Rani', but surely it should have been obvious when, during the Hartnell/Troughton cross-over, even the Doctor's clothes regenerated!

RELIGION: System of faith, sort of contradicted by a programme that explores the universe and finds no Heaven, and which treats believers as impediments to progress. As if that wasn't enough. 'The Dæmons' featured the destruction of a church and provoked complaints from those who somehow couldn't see that it was only an unconvincing replica. For an encore, the production team did it again in 'The Awakening', but this time nobody cared. More recently, the Missing Adventures ran into trouble from the outset, with *Goth Opera* writer Paul Cornell practically being branded the

Anti-Christ in *TV Zone*. Which was nice. The constant appropriation of biblical titles for Dalek and Timewyrm stories must also cause aggravation for the most devout, although Philip Hinchcliffe did consider that 'The Day God Went Mad' was a title too far, substituting the 'The Face of Evil' instead (shouldn't those of us with faces be upset about that?).

RIDICULOUSLY UNREALISTIC SCULPTED MODEL HEADS OF THE FIRST AND SECOND DOCTORS: See 'Dimensions in Time'.

RODAN: Female Gallifreyan traffic controller; no relation to the giant radioactive pteradon that occasionally menaces Tokyo.

ROMANADVORATRELUNDAR: A bit of a daft name for a Time Lord, although being a girl's name it would be. It's a bit of a daft name for a 'Time Lady' too; no wonder Romana decided to call herself Romana. Maybe the Doctor, the Master and the Rani also had really embarassing proper names like Cecilvoratrelundar, Tarquinvoratrelundar and Björk, hence their preference for titles. No? Well, it was just a thought.

RON, BIG: Minor *EastEnders* character played by Ron Tarr. Thanks to his poor showing in the 'Choose your own cliffhanger ending' phone poll, Ron was spared the indignity of having to include 'Dimensions in Time' on his CV.

RUMFORD, PROFESSOR AMELIA: Aged scholar who aided the Doctor and Romana against Cessair of Diplos. She preferred a policeman's truncheon to a man any day of the week, but did agree that there was nothing quite like a sausage sandwich.

RUMOURS: One of the most enjoyable pastimes for a *Doctor Who* fan is to slag off each episode before it's shown. This is greatly facilitated by the fact that, for each genuine piece of news that comes our way, there's at least one totally unfounded rumour. More often than not, this will be of the scare-mongering variety, hinting at upcoming plot twists that would ruin the programme forever and for which the progenitor should be cast into the darkest pit of Hades to burn for eternity. Sometimes, however, the speculation can be more entertaining than the reality. The accompanying list details some of our favourite lies from over the years.

TEN SILLY RUMOURS ABOUT *DOCTOR WHO*

1: The all-American telemovie was to feature a streetwise kid, lots of car chases and a macho Doctor who would cop off with his companion. Oh bugger, it did! Well, at least the idea of a rapping TARDIS console with lips was a bit further off the mark.

2: John Nathan-Turner hinted that the sixth Doctor would be a woman. As intended, this aroused considerable press interest. However, it is without doubt the worst idea ever conceived, and there's no way it should be allowed (unless she's played by Joanna Lumley, in which case we'd be able to invite her to conventions). See also SEXISM.

3: The Brigadier's death in Season Twenty-six in one of several UNIT stories. We were probably meant to be worried when the Brig was, in fact, a bit hurt in 'Battlefield'.

4: The permanent destruction of the TARDIS in 'Frontios'. This would have made subsequent adventures difficult.

5: That man JN-T was at it again, deliberately leaving a document lying around which stated that Colin Baker's first story would be called 'The Doctor's Wife'.

6: 'The King's Demons' was to feature televisions and other anachronistic devices in the thirteenth century.

This comes from no less an impeachable source than *Doctor Who Monthly*'s official preview of the story just before it aired.

7: The sixth Doctor was to be accompanied on his travels by an animatronic cat (K-10?). He got a cat badge instead, but see SPLINX.

8: The middle episode of 'The Happiness Patrol', then called 'The Malapath' for some reason, was going to be entirely animated. This rumour bagan as an April Fool's Joke in the newsletter of a Liverpool telefantasy group, but was picked up and reported as fact by a certain publication.

9: 'The Dark Dimension'. A thirtieth anniversary extravaganza featuring all surviving Doctors. Hardly credible.

10: The story, put about for many years, that there would be a *Doctor Who* movie. This makes us laugh even now. See MOVIE, THE BLOCKBUSTING, MEGA-GROSSING *DOCTOR WHO*.

S

SAND BEAST: Harmless and friendly Didonian creature, brutally slain by that gun-toting warrior woman, Barbara Wright. And people thought the New Adventures version of Ace was bad!

'SCIENCE FICTION ISN'T POPULAR': Famous line employed by BBC 1 Controller Jonathan Powell when attempting to justify the cancellation of *Doctor Who* and the absence of all telefantasy series from his channel. So long as you ignore the viewing figures, the Audience Appreciation Index and the sheer number of fan clubs around the world devoted to SF in its various forms, you can almost start to believe that he had a point. Upon leaving the BBC, Mr Powell became Head of Drama at Carlton Television and thus probably has a better idea of what 'unpopular' means now.

SCRIPT BOOKS: These publications live up to their name by containing scripts for stories of which videos and novelisations are mostly available. Proof that *Doctor Who* fans will buy almost anything. See also 'SHADA' SCRIPT BOOK.

SEASON EIGHTEEN: Amusing omission from *The Doctors – Thirty Years of Time Travel* book.

SERLE, CHRIS: *That's Life* presenter whose likeness was inadvertently used in place of that of Ian Marter on page 37 of *The Dr Who Annual 1976*, in the midst of the classic text story 'The Sinister Sponge'. This landmark book is also notable for the first use of the TARDIS seatbelts.

TEN OVERLOOKED CLASSICS FROM THE WORLD DISTRIBUTORS *DOCTOR WHO ANNUALS*

1. 'The Sinister Sponge' (1976). The women of Inscruta are driving their men insane by making too much noise. The Doctor tries to help but is swallowed by a plant, whilst Harry becomes transparent and Sarah is kidnapped by a displaced inhabitant of Femizor, the gigantic sponge colony in Alpha Mardis 2.
2. 'A Universe Called Fred' (1971). The Doctor and Liz promise to save a doomed subatomic world, then run away without doing anything of the sort. This story is worth reading just for the description of Jon Pertwee's Doctor as 'a pair of dividers in motion'.
3: 'The Nemertines' (1984). Guest-starring the Brigadier (the only character from the past to return in an annual), this not only gives us a glimpse of what a fifth Doctor UNIT story would have been like, it also includes a half-page diagram to explain osmosis, so it's educational too.
4: 'Plague World' (comic strip, 1982). On the planet Publius, the villainous Bemar (a partial anagram of World editor Mae Broadley) sucks the life force from people like Auctor and Stylo (meaning 'writer') to feed the Druden (meaning 'five', as did Pentos, the name of World's parent company). Even the title is only just subtle enough for staff writer Clive Hopwood to get away with it.
5: 'The Fishmen of Kandalinga' (1966). For the first annual only, World could use monsters from the series, except for the only popular ones. We were therefore treated to a second appearance by the ferocious Voord, who were given more depth here than on TV.

Two keys of Marinus also contribute towards making this story a fanboy's dream.

6: 'The Lost Ones' (1966). The second of this year's Vortis-based adventures takes place before the first and, it seems, instead of 'The Web Planet'. Encountering the Menoptera (sic) for the first time, the Doctor accidentally mentions that his kind like to kill butterflies with cyanide and stick pins in them – you know, as you would in that situation. He also meets a group of interplanetary explorers from Atlantis – as if the *Doctor Who* mythos needs another version of that.

7: 'H.M.S. *Tardis*' (1968). This purely historical story (guest-starring Admiral Nelson) is something of a rarity, particularly as it concerns the Doctor's attempt to change the past by making Ben shoot somebody dead.

8: 'Sweet Flower of Uthe' (1981). This SF tale about a computerised war was performed as a play at Manchester's Contact Theatre in 1979. Sadly, the Doctor was removed from the script, although the cast were given proofs of the upcoming annual to work from. The story is more notable, however, for its unique opening sequence, in which the Doctor has to wait outside the TARDIS for Romana to finish in the bathroom. Alarmingly, K9 knows what she's doing and how long, to the nearest tenth of a second, she'll take to finish.

9: 'The Key of Varga' (1982). Although otherwise unremarkable, this holds the distinction of being the first official piece of fifth Doctor fiction. Unfortunately, no one knew that when it was written. World's editors cunningly swapped pictures of Tom Baker for some head shots of Peter Davison (whose costume hadn't yet been designed), still sporting his 'Tristan' hairstyle.

10: 'The Mystery of the *Marie Celeste*' (1970). In defiance of the continuity established during 'The Chase', this story purported to explain the evacuation of the famous ship. Its conclusion has the human crew unwilling to evade certain death by entering the TARDIS, which they think looks a bit scary.

SERVIX: Not one of the Silurians in 'Warriors of the Deep'. However, we know somebody that thought otherwise, and said so in public. Unless he stumps up a fiver by the end of the month, we'll reveal his name in our next reprint. See WALLPAPER for more blackmail.

SEVEN KEYS TO DOOMSDAY, DOCTOR WHO AND THE DALEKS IN THE: Seventies theatrical spin-off, notably primarily for having Simon Jones of *Hitch-Hiker's Guide to the Galaxy* fame lumbering around the stage on a huge pair of stilts. Trevor Martin starred as the Doctor; you may have seen photos of him in costume in *Doctor Who* publications that have a budget for illustrations. Apparently, that was his own hair! Don't worry if you missed the play; just watch 'The Keys of Marinus' and imagine it with some Daleks in.

SEVEN, MARK: Dalek-battling robot star of the sixties series of Dalek books. A pre-cursor of Steve Austin, the Six Million Dollar Man, it was no surprise that the character was revived for the seventies series of Dalek Annuals, when of course Steve Austin, the Six Million Dollar Man, was very popular.

SEX: Activity featured in none of the televised stories and therefore in most New and Missing Adventures, as the Doctor struggles to save the universe with companions copulating all about him. The attitude of most fans is that Ace and Benny can sleep around, Dodo can catch what she likes, and Chris Cwej can father children to his heart's content, so long as the story's canonicity is debatable and the Doctor doesn't get involved. The rumour that the US telemovie might bring such activities to the screen, then, provoked an outcry. See DOCTOR BONK.

SEXISM: Bias of which *Doctor Who* has sometimes been accused, for no better reason than that it features a host of screaming females, often scantily clad, who fall and twist their ankles on the smoothest of surfaces. Attempts have been made to reverse this trend: Zoe was an intelligent, mature young woman who just happened to scream and fall over a lot, while Liz had a keen scientific brain and could converse with the Doctor on his own level when she wasn't being kidnapped or running around in short skirts and thigh-length boots. The bottom line is that the programme's star is an extremely capable man, which means that, for viewer identification, the ideal supporting character will always be a less able woman. Critics have suggested that the casting of a female Doctor would change this (although no one ever asked for a male lead in *Juliet Bravo*). What they fail to realise is that, if regeneration could change a Gallifreyan's sex, then David Campbell and Leela would be in for one hell of a shock.

'SHADA' SCRIPT BOOK: To be found within the same pack as the BBC Video release of 'Shada'. This must have proved an invaluable item for those people who like to read at the same time as watching telly – for once, they wouldn't have to miss anything. Quite a bargain it was too. By cutting down on non-essential luxuries such as decent paper and glossy covers, the Beeb were able to ensure that 'Shada' came out at only twice the price of other single tape releases. Oh, but if only they'd managed to get the diamond logo on the page behind the cover (complete with diamond logo-shaped cut-out hole) instead of on page three, we'd have shelled out the extra cash happily.

SHAGG: Affectionate nickname given by certain fans

to the unnamed character played by Sam West in 'Dimensions in Time'. When the Rani's companion reappeared in a *Doctor Who Yearbook* story also written by David Roden, he had been christened Cyrian, although apparently Rodan had in fact used this name in the original script (yes, of course there was a script!).

SHARPE: Popular historical adventure series that has consolidated Sean Bean's status as a major star, as well as a heartthrob. On the back of *Sharpe*, Bean landed the coveted role of main villain in the Bond blockbuster *Goldeneye*, and the heroic Major himself looks set for a cinematic debut in the proposed film *Sharpe and the Tiger*. Eighth Doctor Paul McGann was in fact the first actor cast as dashing Richard Sharpe, but he damaged the cruciate ligaments in his leg whilst playing football, with only a few minutes of footage in the can. The good news was, of course, that losing out on that role meant he could provide us with an excellent eighth Doctor. That was good news . . . wasn't it, Paul?

SIGMA, TREVOR: Census taker in 'The Happiness Patrol', who decided to compile a register of everybody on the planet Terra Alpha by going around and asking their names. He ended up with a list of 500,000 missing people. Is that so surprising?

SIMPSON, OLLIE: The head of the newest (at time of writing) family on Brookside Close. Isn't that just one of the great things about TV? That in the middle of an innocuous programme like *Brookside* you can suddenly be catapulted to the edge of your seat by the appearance of a new character and the shocking realisation: 'Hey, that's Sir Geoffrey from "The King's Demons"!' See the accompanying list.

TEN SERIES WORTH WATCHING FOR THEIR WEALTH OF *DOCTOR WHO* ACTORS

1: *The Liver Birds*. Having taken a look at the updated version of this Carla Lane sitcom – it was the one that was popular in the seventies with *Who* stars Nerys Hughes from 'Kinda' and Polly James from 'The Awakening' – and noticing the liberties taken with its history, especially the complete removal of one Liver Bird from the continuity (Carole, played by the one who wasn't in *Doctor Who*) and the allocation of her family to one of the remaining Birds, we considered forgiving *Doctor Who* its own continuity gaffes, which are tiny by comparison. But hey, two wrongs don't make a right. So, all things considered, see quite a few other entries.

2: *Keeping Up Appearances*. Average sitcom, elevated by the presence of Geoffrey Hughes, Clive Swift and Judy Cornwell in three of its five starring roles.

3: *The Bill*. Apart from Caroline John's semi-regular appearances as a police doctor, this show is virtually a 'Kinda' reunion, with Simon Rouse, Jeff Stuart and Graham Cole amongst its long-running regular cast (yes, Cole did appear in 'Kinda', he just wasn't credited, all right?). Some actors have said that an episode of *The Bill* comes free with your Equity card, so it's always worth keeping an eye on the guest stars to see who'll turn up next.

4: *Blake's 7*. Being typecast as an SF actor was less of a problem in the days when the BBC made more than one genre series. Paul Darrow, Michael Keating, Jacqueline Pearce, Brian Croucher and Peter Tuddenham were all regulars in Terry Nation's space opera; in return, *Blake's 7* got Colin Baker, Richard Franklin and John Leeson in one-off roles. We won't even attempt to list the many other actors who appeared in both, except to say that they included such *Who* luminaries as Richard Hurndall, Michael Gough and Valentine Dyall. There are thirty-plus others; why not buy the videos and see if you can find them all?

5: *The Avengers*. Another series that seemed to fish in the same talent pool as *Doctor Who*. Standing out from a large crowd are Nick Courtney as an army officer, Anneke Wills, Peter Cushing, Anthony Ainley, Michael Gough and Jon Pertwee.

6: *Emmerdale* (*Farm*). Not a patch on what it used to be in the days when Frazer Hines played the longest-running character in the series (and married *Blake's 7*'s Sally Knyvette) and was joined for a time by Richard Franklin and Wendy Padbury, as well as by Bernard Archard from 'Pyramids of Mars'; and does anyone remember Andrew Burt from 'Terminus' as the original Jack Sugden? (No, nor do we.)

7: *Triangle*. Voted the worst programme in history by TV critics. It starred *Who* semi-regulars Paul Jerricho and Kate O'Mara, the latter of whom got the seafaring soap off to a titillating start by indulging in a spot of topless sunbathing on an obviously freezing deck (obvious, that is, because we could see that the sky was overcast, and not for any other reason you might think of).

8: *EastEnders*. Leslie Grantham, Ian Reddington, Michael Cashman, Tony Caunter, Richard Ireson, Jane How, June Brown, Michael Melia, Brian Croucher, Pamela Salem and Anna Wing were all regulars (see if you can find that lot in your *Programme Guide*), while Sophie Aldred, Peter Purves and Caroline John have all guest-starred. And we won't even mention 'Dimensions in Time'!

9: *Stars in Their Eyes*. No, really. There was this one bloke, Danny Owen, and before his miraculous transformation into former footballer and total babe magnet Julio Iglesias, he told Matthew Kelly that he'd been a robot in *Doctor Who*. He probably was an' all, but if you need to know for certain, check out one of those factual books that give a toss about such trivia.

10: *Coronation Street*. See Bryan Mosley, made famous by his role as Malpha in 'The Daleks' Master Plan', in a different light. Also, anyone who cops off with Rita Sullivan is bound to have been in *Doctor Who* (Mark Eden, William Russell, Donald Gee, John Savident . . .). And, at various points in Corry's past and present: Helen Worth, Geoff Hinsliff, Christopher Coll, Milton Johns, Mary Tamm, Anne Reid, Dicken Ashworth, Geoffrey Hughes, David Daker, Michael Sheard, David Brierley — in three different roles — and doubtless tons more.

'SIX DOCTORS, THE': Working title for what became 'The Five Doctors'. Cor, sounds brilliant. Wonder who they'd have got to make up the numbers ... Peter Cushing? Trevor Martin? Tom Baker? Actually, they did want Colin Baker to reprise his Maxil role from 'Arc of Infinity' ... Nah, it can't be; how could they have known? Spooky.

SIXTH DOCTOR'S COSTUME, THE: Polychromatic disaster reluctantly sported by Colin Baker throughout his short tenure. Colin always said he would have preferred something more austere (plenty to choose from there, then). This costume alone could have prompted Michael Grade to wield his axe. Even John Nathan-Turner now admits it was a mistake, but it was just symptomatic of his predilection for having his regulars wear costumes rather than simply clothes. Apparently for identification purposes, it was really something of a comic book approach. Season Nineteen was the worst culprit, coming before the concerted fan campaign enabled Nyssa to get her pants off; what with Adric's rubber pyjamas and all, it really must have stank in the TARDIS.

SKY RAY SPACE RAIDERS: The updated *Programme Guide* may claim to include the 'missing bits' of *Doctor Who*, but still it omits some of the most absorbing and integral parts of 'unofficial' continuity, as well as 'Dimensions in Time'. Most unforgivably, it neglects Commander Clay's Earth-based 'elite band of Special Duty Space Commandos', the Space Raiders. This courageous group rushed into action to help a version of Doctor Who (sic) who looked a bit like Pat Troughton against the Dalek invasion of Zaos. They relied only on their wits and on modest armaments including an anti-personnel nuclear carbine that could wipe out whole regiments of Daleks without recharging. They travelled in distinctive red and orange ships – craftily disguised as harmless ice lollies – the blueprints of which were so top secret as to be available only to those select few who could garner enough wrappers from Walls' Sky Ray lollies on Earth. Even these drawings were incomplete, deliberately concealing the ships' greatest secret: how they survived the heat of re-entry.

SNATCH: A character in 'Slipback'. Hmmm, wonder what his nickname was at school?

SNOG RATINGS: After 'revealing' that the McGann movie 'boasts super-duper special effects and' – shock! horror! – 'snogging', the *Scottish Daily Record* thought it a good idea to assess the snogability of the previous Doctors. On a scale of one to five Tom Baker and Peter Davison fared best with an impressive four points apiece. Tom apparently 'went through eight assistants', while Peter was 'good with animals'. Coming in third was 'Chubby' Colin Baker with a respectable three; it appears he dropped points because 'he used to shout at pouting Peri' (instead of snogging her, obviously). Both Patrick Troughton and Jon Pertwee only managed to score two. Patrick did however gain another year's worth of stories. But it seems Jon did badly because 'he only had eyes for Bessie'. Bringing up the rear were William Hartnell and Sylvester McCoy, with a measly single point each. We get the feeling that the reporter isn't the world's biggest fan of Sylvester: not only does he find him as kissable as someone who's been dead for over twenty years, he wonders, 'Why was he ever allowed to become a Doctor?' All crucial information for fans of course, but with one vital omission – how snoggable is Paul McGann? Never mind, the *Record* more than made up for that oversight by packing the rest of its two-page spread with facts and figures about the series and its fans. For example, in a section entitled 'The TARDIS Temptresses', we learn that it was 'the Brigadier who uttered the immortal line: "That chap with wings, five rounds, quick fire, sergeant!" ' And, in a valuable insight into the workings of Scottish fandom, it's revealed: 'This week's meeting . . . clashed with a satellite soccer match, and the Doc's disciples had to watch a video of the seventies adventure "The Hand of Fear" with the sound turned down. It didn't matter because they know the story off by heart.' Why aren't we surprised?

SNOTARANS: Another amusing misprint in *The Doctors – Thirty Years of Time Travel* book.

'SO YOU ESCAPED FROM CASTROVALVA': As if to consolidate his eighties image as a sneering, black-clad comic book villain, the Master took to dying at the end of each dastardly plot, only to be resurrected in between episodes. However, whilst Doctor Doom could always offer a concealed jet pack/sidereal journey to a micro-cosmos/intervention by super-intelligent alien beings (delete as appropriate) to explain his return, the Master had bugger all excuse, hence lines like the above. Having been trapped in a collapsing reality, cornered by a dinosaur, stranded on a disintegrating planet and, most tellingly, burnt to death in full view of the Doctor, his feats of escapology have begun to look a bit suspect. Having now witnessed the destruction of the Master's corporeal form, his survival as an energy being, and his abortive attempt to take over a new body which culminated in his being plunged into the Eye of Harmony, we still can't help but feel that, at the end of some future episode, Tony Ainley will step out of the shadows and shout: 'Ta-daaa!'

'SPACK OFF!': The Doctor's single attempt to look hard and mature by swearing, in 'Destiny of the Daleks'. It didn't have much effect, perhaps because of Tom Baker's fluffed delivery. It's difficult to tell what he was actually supposed to say, although we can presumably rule out the obvious. 'Back off' is a possibility, but then where does the 'sp' come from? No, our guess would be that the script said 'Spock off', which for *Who* fans is the most heinous insult imaginable. See also OZXOUGISRA RIZCOICA (if you can find it).

SPAIN: Western European country in which, according to the first Doctor, Ian and Barbara would end up (albeit as burnt-out cinders) if they were to use the Dalek time machine. Many years later, the production team went there for no apparent reason and made 'The Two Doctors'. See FOREIGN LOCATIONS.

SPLINX: Electronic feline assistant of the sixth Doctor in *The Mines of Terror* (see COMPUTER GAMES). Powered by Ulrick Neobium Energiser Cells, Splinx had the ability to make objects larger than herself disappear into her hyperspace load module. What a pity this fantastic character didn't have the benefit of modern computer graphics; had she done so, her active form might have looked a little more like a cat and a lot less like a shaded-in thumb print.

STAIRS: Outdated though it may be, the Daleks' inability to cope with these architectural features remains a mainstay of comedians' routines. Somehow, though, if a Dalek appeared in a stand-up comic's hallway, we don't think he'd be chortling and saying 'I'll just nip up to the bedroom where it's safe'. No, more likely he'd be writhing in the fatal blast field of an alien destructor weapon, wouldn't he? Still, Tom Baker started it, we suppose, by taunting his foes about their lack of manoeuvrability in 'Destiny'. Funny he should pick up on that one flaw, whilst ignoring the fact that the Daleks' casings in that story were mostly unoccupied, all knackered, and tended to wobble when negotiating rough terrain. 'If you're supposed to be the superior race of the universe, why don't you try following me across this loose shale?'

***STAR TREK* FANS:** A group of people infinitely sadder than their *Doctor Who* counterparts. They spend all their time kitted out in full Star Fleet regalia (even under their anoraks) or spouting Klingonese with Mars bars stuck to their foreheads. Not for this bunch the small matter of dealing with reality, and interpersonal relationships just don't come into it, no sir; for Trekkies, happiness is a warm Tribble. To illustrate how out of it they are, we need only mention the death threats and hate mail received by talented British actor Malcolm McDowell following his portrayal of Doctor Sorin in *Star Trek – Generations*. His crime? Simply playing, as scripted, the fictional character responsible for the death of Captain Kirk (who'll probably be back in a couple of films anyway). So far as we can ascertain, David Banks didn't receive a single threatening letter when Adric died. See also FOOTBALL and the accompanying list.

TEN GOOD REASONS WHY *DOCTOR WHO* FANS ARE FAR MORE SANE THAN OTHER INTEREST GROUPS

1: Few people queue overnight to get the best seats at *Doctor Who* conventions; for Cliff Richard concerts, they do.

2: Soap addicts send letters to inform actors of their on-screen spouses' infidelity. Rare are the missives that arrive at the BBC to warn: 'Dear Doctor, The Master is trying to conquer the universe behind your back.'

3: In contrast to the disbanding of Take That, no help lines were needed to console suicidal *Who* fans whenever the programme was cancelled.

4: Admittedly the odd *Doctor Who* T-shirt is available for those sad enough to wear it, but have you tried counting the number of *Red Dwarf* shirts on the market recently? There are thousands of the things, each sporting a line of dialogue from the programme. Someone, somewhere can reproduce the script of an entire episode on his washing line.

5: Unlike the devotees of some religious groups, *Doctor Who* fans wouldn't commit suicide on Tom Baker's say-so. Well, maybe they would, but when John Nathan-Turner cast Richard Briers, there were no public burnings of *The TARDIS Inside Out*, were there?

6: We hear of people naming their sons after football teams, but the day somebody is christened Ian Steven Benjamin James Alistair John Michael Harry K9 Adric Vislor, we'll campaign for the legalisation of euthanasia.

7: Australian fans of *Prisoner: Cell Block H* descended upon the Grundy studios with motorbikes and banners to protest about the death of Franky Doyle. Did this happen in Shepherd's Bush when Katarina bit the dust? No, we don't think it did.

8: Marches and demos by political groups are ten-a-penny, but never once have *Who* fans ventured on to the streets in such a way, not even to protest about the sacking of Colin Baker or to demand the release of 'The Horns of Nimon' on video – laudible causes, both.

9: At time of writing, no university courses in Dalekese are available, yet Trekkies can and do learn Klingon as a second language. Are they all raving nutters or what?

10: The bottom line is this: *Doctor Who* was created to entertain, coins to formalise a system of barter, trains as a method of transport, and stamps as a means of funding the postal service. People find entertainment in all four. Which is the most understandable?

Right, that's off our chests, now on to the next entry:

———————◆———————

STAVROS: Yes matey peeps, it's true, one newspaper did actually get the name of the Dalek's creator embarrassingly wrong (twice!), confusing it with that of Harry Enfield's kebab stand proprietor, or even Kojak's portly underling. Because it was such a nice feature about the series otherwise, we were considering letting the paper remain anonymous and thus sparing its blushes. However, they went on to discuss some of the Doctor's other adversaries like 'the Horrible Snow-men' and, the reporter's personal favourite, 'the Ant Monsters of Zarbi'. Their belief that the first episode was entitled 'An Earthly Child' just swayed it. Sorry, guys at the *Glasgow Herald Weekend Extra*.

STORY CODES, AMUSING: 4Q, of course. Also YYY was 'The Monster of Peladon' ever made? And some people might venture that ZZZ is an appropriate code for 'Planet of the Spiders'.

SUGAR SMACKS: Overtly sweet breakfast cereal, as you may gather from the name. Sweet-toothed or not, when free badges of the third Doctor and friends were included in each box, there was no option for fans but to eat them for breakfast, dinner and tea (that's break-fast, lunch and dinner to you la-di-da Southern readers) if only until the highly prized UNIT badge was dis-covered at the bottom of the packet. That was the theory. In reality, it was usually the case that, several dozen packets later and several teeth ruined in the process, all you had to show for your efforts was a stack of Jo Grant badges and perhaps a Bessie one if you were lucky. The disappointment was further compounded when that git you couldn't stand strutted into school flaunting his UNIT badge and a Dr Who one (his dad probably worked at Kellogg's too, so he didn't even have to eat the bloody Sugar Smacks – twat!).

TEN GREAT *DOCTOR WHO* BADGES

1: Sugar Smacks Master badge. Well, it didn't get a mention above.

2: Sugar Smacks Brigadier badge. Likewise.

3: Zarbi/Venom Grub relief badge produced by Plastoid and part of a set with a Menoptra and a Dalek (naturally). This one's as rare as rocking horse dung and almost as appealing.

4: 'TARDIS Commander' badge: produced for the BBC Special Effects Exhibition in 1972. A similar product appeared a few years later at the Blackpool Exhibition. It has to be said that even with a question-mark tank top or a long scarf and some celery, you can't be considered a fully dressed Doctor wannabe without the addition of one of these collector's items.

5: Diamond logo on blue background. It seems the BBC have lost all their proper diamond logos: whenever they need to feature the programme in *Radio Times* or somewhere, they always have to stick a photo of this badge on the article.

6: 'BBC *Doctor Who* Exhibition 21 Years at Longleat 1973–1994'. As good an excuse for a badge as any we suppose.

7: 'K9 says Save Energy'. Photo-badge produced by the Energy Conservation Unit County Architects Dept, County Hall, Beverly in 1982. One to look out for.

8: 'I'm on Target with *Doctor Who*'. A more considered W H Allen promo tag line than their other, rather disappointing effort, 'I'm a *Doctor Who* reader'. For some reason, their successors have never taken up the baton by producing a badge that reads 'I'm a Virgin *Doctor Who* fan'.

9: 'Doctor Who USA'. At the time, just another piece of merchandise, along with key-rings, T-shirts, etc, sold on the mid-eighties touring Doctor Who Exhibition. Now it's almost like this was a frightening prophesy of things to come.

10: The HMV badge, free with the US telemovie video. Well, we've had the diamond logo, the neon logo and even the crappy McCoy era logo on badges, so it's about time the Pertwee version had its turn.

SWEET CIGARETTES: You can't seem to get these anymore – can't think why. Perhaps after kids have spent their pocket money on the real thing, they can't afford fakes too. Anyway, back in 1965 Cadet Sweets issued a set of fifty 'Doctor Who and the Daleks' cards to go with their kiddie fags. Great they were, too. Gloriously illustrated by Richard Jennings (of TV 21 Dalek strip fame), they had the first Doctor encounter the Daleks, the Voord (blimey, Terry Nation was quids in there) and the best Doctor Who character never to have appeared in Doctor Who, the globe-headed Golden Emperor Dalek (of TV 21 Dalek strip fame).* If after reading this you're thinking of collecting the Cadet cards, don't. Although cheaper than a sparkly Cornerstone premium trading card, odds (that's a technical term for individual cards) are damned expensive and the cost of a full set all but transcends the laws of mathematics. Incidentally, Goodies sweets reissued some of the cards in the eighties, but when someone pointed out that the Doctor wasn't a white-haired old bloke anymore, they stopped.

* Okay, so maybe the globe-headed White Emperor Dalek seen in 'Remembrance' was inspired by this comic strip character, but it was actually more reminiscent of one of those household air freshners – you know, the white globe-shaped ones.

SYNCHRONICITY: Technobabble used in 'The Ghosts of N-Space' to cover the fact that the entire plot hinged on a pretty enormous coincidence, to wit: a chance meeting between the Brigadier, Sarah Jane and Jeremy Fitzoliver in Italy. Perhaps it's a Time Lord gift that, when the Doctor is around, the most unlikely things occur with startling regularity. Without the one in three million chance that Eldrad would survive dispersal, the Nunton Experimental Complex would never have been menaced by a big hand. Conversely, had the Brigadier met himself during any other millisecond on Mawdryn's ship, the Doctor would be dead. And then there's 'The Green Death' and its example of serendipity, which is of course one more way of saying 'walloping great plot convenience'.

T

TA: The planet on which the Issigri Mining Company is based; affectionately known to its inhabitants as 'Dalek Cutaway', perhaps?

TALKING BOOKS: If you've bought this book, you're obviously very easily amused. So, if you really want a good laugh, buy the BBC Audio Collection versions of Target books read by various Doctors. Speaking of Talking Books, Paul McGann is reading some *Sharpe* novels – well, it's about as close as he's going to get (see *SHARPE*).

TARAN BEAST: Terrifying inhabitant of the planet Tara, whose threat was somewhat understated during our one glimpse of it. Romana, fortunately, was wise enough to steer clear of the monstrosity; a lesser person might have fatally under-estimated its abilities, lulled by the creature's deceptively comedic appearance.

TARDIS TELEPATHIC CIRCUITS: If the bit about 'a Time Lord gift' isn't convincing, how about this handy device, which enables the Doctor's English-speaking companions to understand and communicate in all manner of alien languages from Dalekese to erm, Cyberish. Presumably it was slightly damaged when the TARDIS took the battering that caused the sixth

Doctor to regenerate, as he was subsequently perceived to be speaking with a pronounced Scottish accent.

TARDIS TIN: As if to disguise the fact that they'd chosen 'The Trial of a Time Lord' to commemorate *Doctor Who*'s thirtieth anniversary, BBC Video released it in this distinctive packaging. Ardent completists had the option of buying seven versions, at thirty quid a throw, each picturing a different Doctor on the base. For the rest of us, one Colin Baker tin was more than adequate and could also be used, sans videos, as a rather attractive lunchbox (as could the tin's less novel counterpart from the Dalek video set, of which only four versions were issued). The most prudent fans, however, were those who went into Woolworths and bought the videos tinless for a fiver.

TARDIS VIDEO CABINET: An indispensable item of merchandise. Granted, a four-foot police box might look a bit silly in the front room, but at least you can hide those 'uniform edition' BBC videos away. Perhaps it's just as well, though, that some of the *Doctor Who* logos point sideways while others point upwards, sometimes with a '30th Anniversary' banner attached, and that the BBC logo switches alarmingly in design and location on the spines. Just imagine if the Beeb had maintained a uniformity with their *Doctor Who* video releases: there'd be a common desire to display the set proudly, and a common worry of what the hell to do with that special edition 'Silver Nemesis' in all its metallic, snot-green glory?*

* *In all fairness to BBC Video, they did replace the cover for their very first release, 'Revenge of the Cybermen', which came out initially in a huge box made of brittle plastic adorned with pictures of Cybermen from 'Earthshock' and topped off with the neon logo.*

TARGET: Former imprint of publishers W H Allen which, over many years, released novelisations of most of the *Doctor Who* scripts not written by Douglas Adams. These varied in size from, typically, 144 pages (for a two-parter) to 144 pages (for a ten-parter), which usually meant that most of the story was missing or that it should have been. A notable exception was 'The Daleks' Master Plan', which was split into two volumes to prevent either one from being too heavy. See also *JUNIOR DOCTOR WHO*, and in fact many other entries, including . . .

TARGET BOOK SPINES: Nobody, but nobody, wanted Target to start numbering the spines of their *Doctor Who* novelisations. To collectors, it was the worst idea since Marvel Comics stopped numbering their issues of *Doctor Who Weekly*. It meant that 'Kinda' came right after 'Snakedance' on the shelf (they realised in time to swap the release schedules, but not to change the numbers!) and that there was no book 106 for over a year when 'Vengeance on Varos' was delayed. Did someone really think it was a good idea to read the things in alphabetical order? Honestly, it's hard enough to find a Target/W H Allen/Virgin *Doctor Who* book without a knackered spine; you don't need any more aggro.

TERILEPTILS' HUNTING KNIVES: Not seen on screen; however, thanks to the BBC Audio release of 'The Power of the Daleks', we do know that they're slightly less sharp than the air on Vulcan.

THATCHED ROOFS: Their incongruous appearance in 'Terror of the Zygons' made it obvious that genuine Scottish locations had not been utilised. However, only pedantic fans from north of the border are in the slightest bit bothered about this budgetary necessity, which after all did make the landscape look prettier.

THATCHER, MRS: Popular Prime Minister of the eighties (hey, she must have been popular with someone – she kept getting bloody well re-elected). Margaret Thatcher might well have been the female Prime Minister predicted in 'Terror of the Zygons', but then again she might not – who cares? In Richard Franklin's 1984 Edinburgh Fringe production, *Recall UNIT or the Great T-Bag Mystery*, Maggie ended up in a teabag, having been reduced by the Master's Tissue Compression Eliminator. This being a bit of a political satire type thing, we suspect that the T-Bag reference was a veiled insult aimed at the Iron Lady (T-Bag = Mrs T, old bag). Richard Franklin might think that, but we couldn't possibly comment. Thatch's last *Doctor Who* appearance to date was in *The Ultimate Adventure*. Unlike *Recall UNIT*, this stageplay had a budget and could afford someone to play her (Judith Hibbert). We also suspect there may have been subtle Thatcher analogies in *Turlough and the Earthlink Dilemma* and 'The Happiness Patrol', but we couldn't swear to it.

'THE ANORAKS HAVE LANDED': Perceptive comment from Paul McGann following his first encounter with *Doctor Who* fans.

'THE MEMORY CHEATS': Arguably producer John Nathan-Turner's most popular catchphrase, narrowly beating 'Stay tuned', 'No comment' and 'I have been persuaded to stay'. The gist of this remark is that if you believed his episodes to be worse than his predecessors', you must have forgotten how bad the earlier ones were. This can't be true as, some fifteen years after the event, we still consider 'Time-Fight' to be a load of old cack.

'THERE'S NOTHING YOU CAN DO TO STOP THE CATHARSIS OF SPURIOUS MORALITY': Popular line of dialogue spouted by the Valeyard in 'The Trial of a Time Lord' part fourteen. Roughly translated, it means 'You can't stop me from killing those Time Lords out there'. The Doctor, of course, was able to confound this prophecy by triggering 'a ray-phase shift'. Strange how the casual viewer can rarely foresee such obvious resolutions.

'THE THING ABOUT THE CYBERMEN IS THAT THEY HAVE IRON WILLS': Accidental double entendre spoken by Cyberleader actor (and occasional Doctor) David Banks at the first Manopticon convention. Well, we still think it's funny.

THREE OF CLUBS: In an effort to broaden the horizons of recent *Doctor Who* merchandise, which seems to have consisted mainly of sets of trading cards, one company had the imaginative notion to stick some numbers and suits on to them and call them playing cards. Quite sensibly, they dedicated a suit to each of the first four Doctors: clubs for Hartnell, spades for Troughton, diamonds for Pertwee and hearts for Tom Baker, with photos from the relevant eras adorning each card. So quite why they included a shot of Zoe from 'The Dominators' amidst those featuring the Zarbi, Ian and Susan, etc, is uncertain. Perhaps they looked at the trump cards for inspiration and thought it was traditional to bugger at least one of them up?

TINSEL: Vital component of Karfelon technology.

TITLE SEQUENCES, ALTERNATIVE: For 'alternative' read 'not really good enough to use'. One of these can be seen on *The Pertwee Years* video accompanied by an alternative version of the theme music (in this instance, for 'alternative' read 'too bloody awful to use' – not that this stopped them in later years). Another, you may have seen in part in trailers for Season Seventeen; a bit of an odd combination it was too, with the mighty diamond logo done as a kind of red neon affair. Come to think of it, it was quite nice actually, and far less deserving of the alternative designation than say the one with Sylvester McCoy's face painted silver and the logo that wouldn't print on magazine covers. There are apparently different versions of this sequence too, including the unfinished one accidentally broadcast during 'Time and the Rani', but quite honestly, who could care less?

TOM BAKER DOLL: A great idea of Denys Fisher's, producing a set of *Doctor Who* based dollies for the fans to play with; it's just a pity they weren't better in execution. The lack of similarity between Tom Baker and the fourth Doctor doll has prompted people to suggest that the heads were actually made for the Mike Gambit figure, intended to join Purdey in a *New Avengers* range of larger dolls. However, this theory fails to take into account the fact that it looks even less like Gareth Hunt than it does Tom Baker. The companion Leela doll is obviously based on Louise Jameson, but with one noticeable difference – it is rather too well endowed in the bosom department. No disrespect to Miss Jameson, however: the enormous Peri-sized hooters on this doll make Pamela Anderson seem flat-chested by comparison. If they'd made it in the correct proportions, they could have added an extra figure to the range using the plastic they'd saved. Then perhaps a Zygon could have joined the Dalek (almost perfect, but for a great big blue eye-stalk, Cyberman (yes, the one with the nose), Giant Robot (with detachable shoulder sections, designed to get lost), K9 (very good) and the TARDIS (not very good) in this memorable set.

TOM-TIT: Is there any point pretending we've included this for any reason other than that it's got the word 'tit' in it?

'TOO BROAD AND TOO DEEP FOR THE SMALL SCREEN': Boastful claim on the backs of the New Adventures. We can think of a few more suitable adjectives, but they've removed the offending blurb now so we won't bother to list them.

TOOLKIT: How we all chuckled at those implements that comprised the Doctor's toolkit in 'Earthshock', lovingly detailed and described in *The Doctor Who Technical Manual*. Little did we suspect that, a mere thirteen years later, every last one of them would be rebuilt for 'The US Telemovie with the Pertwee Logo'. It's a shame, though, that after they went to all the trouble of constructing a new sonic screwdriver from the manual's specifications, Sylvester McCoy used it incorrectly, rendering all that attention to detail meaningless. And we still don't know what a neutron ram is, as when the Doctor asked Grace to pass it, she picked up a magnetic clamp instead and whacked him over the head with it (although as the magnetic clamp is vaguely mallet-shaped, perhaps we did at least find out what that is for).

TRADING CARDS: A collector's nightmare. You can't just buy these things. Oh no, you have to get lots of little packs until you build up a set, or more likely end up with no number 6 and twenty copies of number 41, for instance. With a recent resurgence of this hobby, it was inevitable that *Doctor Who* would be dragged on to the bandwagon. Unfortunately, fans were denied the all-new artwork of *The X-Files* and the Marvel characters, to be given instead the same old photos with the same old facts on the back. Modern-day manufacturers have also found a novel way of ripping us off: whereas their predecessors guaranteed that each card was printed in equal amounts, it's now somehow acceptable to guarantee that they aren't. Your collection is not complete without a plethora of rare 'bonus' cards, usually the same as the normal ones but with cheap pieces of foil stamped on to them. And when you finally get cards 1–110 and the associated extras, they bring out 111–220 and you have to go through the whole rigmarole again. Or not.

TRANSVESTISISM: The Doctor revealed a hitherto unseen talent for disguise (we don't count putting a shawl over his head and talking in a squeaky voice in 'The Highlanders') in 'The Green Death'. Taking inspiration from many a British comedian out for a guaranteed cheap laugh, he successfully transformed himself into an old cleaning woman. Possibly influenced by the great man's female impersonation, those normally butch soldiers Yates and Benton indulged in a spot of cross-dressing themselves when the authorities saw fit to *Recall UNIT*. The Doctor's real female companions sometimes got in on the act too: Vicki, Polly and Sarah Jane were all mistaken for boys whilst visiting the past. Our forebears, it seems, were not only prudish about dress codes, but also stupid or blind or both. 'Hmmm, it's got long hair, a pretty face, curvaceous thighs and two big wobbly things on its front. But, hang on a mo . . . it's wearing pants! Must be a chap, then.' We don't think so.

TRAVELS WITHOUT THE TARDIS: This eighties

Target non-fiction book by a couple of Americans was promoted as a guide to the locations used over the years for the filming of *Doctor Who*. We must assume then that it was a comprehensive directory of the quarries of Southern England.

TREMAS: Nyssa's father, whose own parents should have known better than to give him a name that was anagrammatical of 'Master'. Unable to resist this lexical lure, the bearded nasty took over Tremas's body and went on to destroy the entire constellation of his homeworld, Traken. (Yes, we know what you're all thinking: 'Bruce' isn't an anagram of 'Master', so this theory falls down. But we never did learn his surname, did we? Bet it was 'Stream', or 'Sterma' or something.)

TEN CLEVER ANAGRAMS USED IN *DOCTOR WHO*

1: That fiendishly fiendish fiend the Master was at it again, with the impenetrable alias 'Sir Gilles Estram' covering his devillish exploits in thirteenth-century England.

2: The Master's real-life counterpart hid behind more noms-de-plume than his character. Credits for Neil Toynay (Tony Ainley) and James Stoker (Master's Joke) concealed his participation in 'Castrovalva' and 'The King's Demons' respectively. The more desperate Leon Ny Taiy was used for 'Time-Flight'; since the Master had no reason to become the oriental Kalid, one might uncharitably suggest that the anagram came first and the script was shaped to accommodate it.

3: 'The Leisure Hive' featured the vicious alien Foamasi, which probably got the writer on to the hit list of a certain Italian family.

4: We still can't figure out why Davros believed that, having encased the Kaled people in Mark III travel machines, he should also rearrange the letters in their name.

5: Roy Tromelly was Terry Molloy's attempt at 'doing an

Ainley' for 'Remembrance of the Daleks', disguising the fact that the Emperor Dalek was Davros in disguise. But why was this necessary? When Molloy played Russell in 'Attack of the Cybermen', nobody expected him to peel away a latex mask, nor to whip off his pants and reveal the familiar balls of a Dalek casing beneath.

6: The main villain in the *Companions of Doctor Who* novel *Turlough and the Earthlink Dilemma* was christened Rehctaht, which is in fact a subtle anagram of a then topical figure's name. See if you can work out who it is.

7: As if to confirm the place of anagrams within the *Companions* series, *Harry Sullivan's War* sent its eponymous hero undercover as Laury L Varnish. It also featured one Samantha Shire, who didn't turn out to be Sarah Jane Smith, presumably because she was missing one 'J' to make it work.

8: Crinoth rearranged becomes the Greek city of Corinth: the one true anagram in 'The Horns of Nimon', alongside such near-misses as Skonnos/Knossos and Aneth/Athens. The story's roots are therefore just a tad exposed.

9: The metaphorical Holy Grail for which the Rani searched on Lakertya turned out to be Loyhargil.

10: The Missing Adventure title *Managra* is a deliberate anagram of, erm, anagram. Similarly, the Season Twenty-two extravaganza 'Timelash' can be rearranged to form the words 'lame shit'; however, this is probably just a coincidence. By another astonishing fluke, 'The Time Monster' is an anagram of 'total bollocks'. Well, actually it isn't. But it should be.

'TRIAL OF A TIME LORD, THE' PARTS FIVE TO EIGHT (AKA 'MINDWARP'): Was it just us, or did you find aspects of this Trial segment a bit confusing too? Apparently the writer thought it was up to the script-editor to iron out the baffling bits, while the script-editor thought the responsibility for that kind of thing lay with the writer. Well, that explains it then.

'TRIAL OF A TIME LORD, THE' PART FOUR-TEEN (THE SAWARD VERSION): The sad and untimely death of Robert Holmes left the longest and dullest *Doctor Who* story ever without its long-awaited conclusion. With no *Who* writers of Holmes's calibre available – because there aren't any – it was left to script-editor Eric Saward to have the first crack at bringing the Doctor's interminable trial to a close. Basically, what happened in his version was this. The Doctor is sinking in mud (okay so far). He takes time out from worrying about this to have an argument with the Valeyard and to slag off the childish nature of the illusions, apparently forgetting that they seem to be doing the trick. After a bit more witty banter, the Master arrives and pulls the Doctor free. Meanwhile, in the court room set, the Inquisitor reveals that the High Council have resigned *en masse* and Gallifrey has been thrown into turmoil. She doesn't bother to elaborate on this bit of news. It's now time for another of the Valeyard's fiendish illusions, and this one's a corker. The Doctor and Mel are caught in a circular corridor. Destined to go round in circles forever, they even begin to think in annular terms: 'We're becom-ing obsessed by circumnabulation. Added to which a degree of circumloquacious circumvolution has edged into our vocabulary.' Once this dawns on the Doctor, however, the illusion is shattered and Mel, a clever part of it, vanishes too. Then, the startling revelation of the episode: the Valeyard has access to a Time Vent, which can have devastating consequences for the time continuum if left open for more than 72 seconds (!), and because, as Glitz puts it, he's 'got the hump about dying', he's gonna use it! Back to the courtroom drama, as the Inquisitor decides that the simplest way to prevent this is to despatch the Valeyard retroactively by having the Doctor killed. Hang on, isn't that what the

Valeyard wants anyway? There's some unfathomable logic here which suggests that, if he has some contract signed by the High Council, he can have his earlier self killed and then 'inherit' the remaining regenerations. The Master is assigned to execute the Doctor but doesn't on the grounds that it will ruin his anti-establishment image (he comes across as a bit of a hero in this script; hard to believe but it's almost as if Saward prefers him to the sixth Doctor). And then it's time for the dramatic conclusion. By hurling a few insults, the Doctor provokes the Valeyard into opening the Time Vent, into which they both fall and which may become their prison for all eternity. Glitz closes the Time Vent – with seconds to spare, naturally. Gosh! Cracking stuff, eh? What a pity this script went when Eric did. Fortunately, though, it was replaced by an equally wonderful effort from Pip and Jane Baker.

TURGIDS: Humanoid adversaries who imprisoned the Doctor and a presumably regenerated Romana in a solid steel dungeon. Our heroes escaped by using a Time Lord device known as the TARDIS Tuner which, as Romana so astutely pointed out, was just a radio with a silly name. This one-page advertising strip concluded by offering 'all space kids' the chance to buy their own 'amazing *Dr Who* radio'. As well as being emblazoned with the diamond logo, it could emit flashing lights and squealing noises (sorry, we mean its 'time warp bleeper', of course). So uninteresting was this piece of merchandise, in fact, that the advert resorted to expounding the 'mind blowing' properties of its volume control and tried to tempt consumers with its 'sliding door for battery supplies'. It is notable that, even in the comic strip, the TARDIS Tuner overcomes the Turgid guard by sending him to sleep.

TWELVE: The number of regenerations afforded to a Time Lord – and yet, according to the eighth Doctor, his number of lives as well. Fortunately, the Time Lord gift of translation stretched to correcting this slip of the script. Good job Grace Holloway can't read lips.

***TWIN DILEMMA, THE* – ORIGINAL BOOK COVER:** Wanting something special to adorn the front of the sixth Doctor's debut adventure novelisation, Target went to the trouble of getting Andrew Skilleter to paint a rather striking portrait of Colin Baker and then printing up the covers, complete with gold embossed logo, without asking Colin if he minded seeing his face on them. He did. Not to worry; at least Target now had something decent to send convention organisers requesting auction items, instead of covers we already had at home, and with books inside too.

TYTHONIAN AMBASSADOR: Hugely over-endowed monster that received oral stimulation from the Doctor in 'The Creature from the Pit'. Yes, we know it's crude, but you watch the story – it's as blatant as it gets. See also CENTAURI, ALPHA, if you must.

U

ULTIMATE ADVENTURE, THE – FITTING IT INTO CONTINUITY: At first, this was no problem: there's no reason why, after regaining control of the TARDIS, the third Doctor couldn't have got up one morning in UNIT HQ, taken off for a couple of centuries' worth of adventuring including those with Crystal and the French bloke, and still been back for breakfast. However, things became a bit harder to accommodate when Colin Baker took over the part, even though the narrative could have fitted neatly into the period just before the Doctor first met Mel, or just after he first met Mel, or both. It's unlikely that he could have had the same adventure twice without noticing (not counting 'Remembrance of the Daleks' and 'Silver Nemesis', of course), thus requiring one version or other to be 'fired' from the canon. So, is *The Ultimate Adventure* a third or a sixth Doctor story? We have to conclude that it is neither: in fact, it's a David Banks story set within the parallel *Doctor Who* stageplay universe: a universe where the Vervoids are not extinct, where the Daleks look even cheaper than the TV ones, and where people burst into song at the drop of a sonic screwdriver. Banks's beige-suited, Greenpeace T-shirt-wearing Doctor is actually the fifth incarnation within that universe, having succeded Trevor Martin's fourth (the latter being seen – via inserted filmed images – to regenerate from Jon Pertwee at the beginning of *Doctor Who and the Daleks in the Seven Keys to Doomsday*. Yeah, and if you believe that, you probably think 'Dimensions in Time' follows on from 'Shada'!

UMBRELLA SEASON: Fan jargon applying uniquely to Season Sixteen, which featured the Doctor's ongoing exploits to recover the Key to Time (as opposed to, say, Season Twenty-four, in which he used his umbrella a lot). Such an arrangement precludes the BBC from repeating just one or two stories (but they did), Target from releasing an incomplete set of novelisations (but they did), and Virgin from fitting a Missing Adventure between episodes (but they did). At least BBC Enterprises got it right, bringing out each story in order and with a nice painting of – erm – something across the spines too. *Doctor Who* has also had two mini-umbrella seasons-within-seasons: the E-space trilogy gave the Doctor the chance to land on planets and fight monsters as always, but to quote negative co-ordinates when he got there; and the Black Guardian/Turlough stories were a novel way of introducing a mould-breaking new companion and giving him space to develop into someone who, henceforth, could get tied up each week and ask questions.

UNDERPANTS, *DOCTOR WHO*: Funnily enough, although we often see fans decked out in question-mark pullovers and officially licensed long scarves, we rarely, if ever, see them with Tom Baker and the Daleks emblazoned across their genitalia. Of course, it isn't so surprising that collectors are reluctant to get their rare and valuable keks covered in all manner of horrid stains.

UNFAMILIAR MONSTERS, MANKIND'S UN-ERRING ABILITY TO GUESS THE IDENTITIES

OF: This inexplicable talent became evident when a Martian warrior was thawed out of a block of ice and the humans, naturally, christened it an 'Ice Warrior'. Imagine their surprise when this turned out to be the very name by which the Martians knew themselves. Later on, we witnessed the discovery of reptilian men from the Eocene period; UNIT called them Silurians and, despite the inaccuracy of the label, this turned out to be correct as well. On a roll now, the authorities declared that if they were fighting devils from the sea then they had to be called Sea Devils. Right again.

UNFEASIBLY LONG MULTI-COLOURED SCARF: An item of clothing famously worn by the wild-eyed Bohemian that was the fourth Doctor. Often imitated by sad bastards, who usually get the colours wrong. A fine example of a fan scarf was found by the eighth Doctor in a hospital locker; someone must have been attending the Millennium fancy-dress celebrations as the popular TV character Doctor Who.

UNIT: A specialist military force dedicated to the protection of Earth and the thwarting of alien invasions. Although a highly secret organisation it was still possible to join UNIT, and so aid mankind's struggle against the forces of evil, by sending 25p to *Doctor Who Weekly*. See also UNIT SECURITY CODES.

UNIT ADVENTURES, PROBLEMATIC TIMESCALE OF: Nice as it was to see Nick Courtney again in 'Mawdryn Undead', did it have to be in a story that was written for William Russell? Continuity freaks are still trying to cope with the impact of the Brigadier's unlikely decision to leave UNIT and become a schoolteacher. More importantly, the 1977 setting stuffs up almost everything that was established about Earth's history in *Doctor Who*. Some people have done their best to claim that 'Mawdryn' was in fact correct, and that the UNIT stories of the early seventies were really contemporaneous. They cite evidence such as the TV broadcast of *The Clangers* seen in 'The Sea Devils' (as this never happened during the eighties). However, as Sarah says the less ambiguous line 'I came from 1980' in 'Pyramids of Mars', we tend towards the view that a giant cock-up has been made.

TEN POPULAR CONTINUITY ERRORS TO PICK OVER AT YOUR LEISURE AND SLAG OFF WITH YOUR FRIENDS

1: The Silver Jubilee backdrop to 'Mawdryn Undead', which shot UNIT continuity to pieces and split fandom down the middle.

2: The second Doctor recalling in 'The Five Doctors' the events that led to his regeneration.

3: IM Forman: the simple spelling mistake that rendered laughable the programme's attempts to return to its roots in 'Remembrance of the Daleks'.

4: The monsters in 'Warriors of the Deep' referring to themselves as 'Silurians', despite never having been called that (see also UNFAMILIAR MONSTERS, MANKIND'S UNERRING ABILITY TO GUESS THE IDENTITIES OF).

5: Marc Cory's dying message from 'Mission to the Unknown', which played back in 'The Daleks' Master Plan' had been mysteriously altered.

6: The two opposing explanations for the Big Bang, given in 'Terminus' and 'Slipback'.

7: Three different versions of Atlantis, each suffering its own destruction.

8: The Doctor leaving with Mel at the end of 'The Trial of a Time Lord', despite not having yet met her.

9: 'The Ghosts of N-Space' complicates everything, as 'N-Space' was defined as being something entirely different in 'Full Circle' (the executive producer for which was Barry Letts, who wrote 'The Ghosts of N-Space').

10: The Cybermen in 'Earthshock' recalling the events of 'Revenge of the Cybermen', which took place in their own future. Someone should have been shot for that one!

UNIT PASSES: As any true fan knows, most of these were yellow. However, the Doctor's pass was seen in only one story during the seventies, and this was the now chromatically-challenged 'The Mind of Evil'. When John Nathan-Turner wanted to resurrect the object, then, for 'Battlefield', it sparked off a bout of research, undertaken in the cause of ensuring strict accuracy. Nice to know this sort of attention to detail exists. Now, if only they'd thought to check the dating of those UNIT stories, we'd be happy.

UNIT SECURITY CODES: Vital defensive weapons in the raging war against extra-terrestrial life forms. Where bombs, jets and five rounds rapid were prone to failure, these simple substitution codes were bound to throw the enemy into sheer panic. They were used to disseminate crucial information to those selfless readers of *Doctor Who Weekly* who had undertaken to become honorary UNIT members. 'Be on the alert against Auton invasion,' reads a typical communiqué. 'Report a sudden suspicious appearance of any large successful plastics companies in your sector.' The comic's regular 'UNIT Hotline' page also proved to be a mine of fascinating information, from detailed stats on potential alien hazards to blurred pictures of fuzzy shapes in the sky that purported to be spaceships. For some reason, this vital service was eventually discontinued; who knows, perhaps UNIT served its purpose and Earth once again became a safe place on which to live. We have, however, found one last use for the UNIT codebook: by encrypting the following entry into Security Code Green, we can ensure that our editors will be unable to censor it.

OZXOUGISRA RIZCOICA: Ug keaxz'g xaaw xe rezc ice gtig *Kehgem Lte* lix i doma dmec-miwwa, ozxorruak sn dmepizuguax izk ihhadgisra pem hturkmaz. Gtaz Uiz Wimgam'x zefaruxiguez ep 'Gta Azawn ep gta Lemrk' dmefebak i xgemw lugt ugx oggamrn cmigougeox oxa ep gta lemk 'sixgimk', izk pizkew lix mehbak. Zel, ep heomxa, ug ux dmihguhirrn i majoumawazg ep gta Zal izk Wuxxuzc Ikfazgomax gtig gtan xteork uzhroka 'xtug', 'p**b' izk egtam aqiwdrax ep aqgmawa mokazaxx. Gta puzir xgmil, telafam, lix 'Gta Ctexgx ep Z-Xdiha', ltuht paigomak smeikhixg *Lte*'x pumxg zioctgn lemk ('helxtug'). I duaha ep uzzehazha tix saaz xgeraz pmew gta lemrk, izk gtama'x ze aqhoxa pem ug ig irr.

'UP IN ARMS': State attributed to fandom by the media, whenever bad news is received about the show. This can range from the eighteen-month suspension to the casting of light entertainment stars in serious roles. Whatever happens, the fans are outside BBC Television Centre like a shot and waving their sonic screwdrivers in disgust.

URBANKANS: Alien race constantly described as 'froglike', though the reality was that they weren't in the slightest – except in the sense of being green. Applying the same logic, it follows that the Incredible Hulk, John Steed's vintage Bentley, and lime-flavoured opal fruits must be considered 'froglike'.

V

VASELINE: Even the judicious use of this petroleum-based ointment upon camera lenses couldn't disguise the fact that the costumes in 'The Web Planet' were amusing, nor that one Zarbi walked head-first into a camera. *Doctor Who* reference works used to describe this serial as a bold experiment, praising it for being the only story without any humanoid characters beyond the four regulars. They've not said much since we all saw it on video, have they?

VERVOIDS: See MONSTERS THAT LOOK VERY RUDE.

VIBRO-CHAIR, THE: The uses of this potentially interesting futuristic device were sadly not expanded upon when it was briefly seen in 'The Ice Warriors'. Perhaps it was from the same manufacturers as Sutekh's chair with its movable hand attachment.

VID-PHONES: One of the enduring mysteries of the *Doctor Who* universe is why the Sontarans – a clone race – felt the need to develop this technology.

TEN HANDY TIPS FOR *DOCTOR WHO* MONSTERS

1: Sontarans. If you can't afford a vid-phone and feel a bit left out, an ordinary phone with a mirror hung above it makes a convincing and cheap alternative.

2: Daleks. Should someone in an incongruous-looking blue box wearing silly clothes and accompanied by a cute bimbo arrive on the planet you're attempting to conquer, leave immediately – you've no chance.

3: Vervoids. Reduce the risk of becoming extinct by keeping away from genocidal maniacs in multi-coloured patchwork coats . . . whoops, too late.

4: Cybermen. The ingenuity of Cyber technology, coupled with the application of a little silver paint, is all that's needed to transform an ordinary child's air-flow ball into a formidable, yet cheap, weapon of destruction.

5: Yeti. Avoid unsightly body hair by persuading the so-called Great Intelligence to devise a more sensible form for his invasion forces.

6: Zygons. Make wads of cash by opening a souvenir shop at Loch Ness and selling official Skarasen merchandise.

7: Sea Devils. A woolly jumper worn in the winter months makes a less draughty alternative to a string vest (yes, we know, a crap and obvious one, but it had to be done).

8: Vulpanans. As special lighting effects appear to work as well as moonlight in inducing your transformation into bloodthirsty, crazed were-beasts, it is advisable that invitations to the theatre are politely declined – unless you are prepared to face a lengthy prison sentence, or hefty dry-cleaning bills from gore-splattered survivors.

9: Ice Warriors. Be sure to check that any installations you have to take over during your proposed conquest of Mankind don't have easily accessible thermostat switches. If they do, smash the buggers post-haste. Alternatively, use them to your advantage by changing your name to 'Fire Warriors' and wearing Bermuda shorts and knotted hankies on your heads. The Earthling scum will assume you love it hot and see to it that the temperature is kept to an absolute minimum. Sorted!

10: Zarbi. Give it up guys – you're rubbish!

VIEWMASTER: A lump of plastic which, with cardboard discs inserted, produces 3-D images vastly superior to those seen in 'Dimensions in Time'. Amongst its view reels, *Doctor Who* has been represented by collections of scenes from 'Full Circle' and 'Castrovalva'. For a few weeks, the former was packaged in an attractive box featuring Daleks that were neither appropriate nor paid for. Enjoyable piece of eighties kitsch, and the *Starliner* never looked so good. But if only they'd done 'Planet of Fire' . . .

VULCAN: It is, sadly, a common fallacy that 'The Power of the Daleks' featured a world called Vulcan before *Star Trek* used the name for the homeworld of that pointy-eared bloke. In fact the US series got there first by a few weeks. However, both series obviously lifted the name from the theoretical planet once believed to share Mercury's orbit, which is surely the only relevant point to make. Ah well, at least we had Voga before *The Hitch-Hiker's Guide to the Galaxy* did.

VWORP, VWORP: Onomatopoeic representation of the raucous wheezing, groaning sound that invariably accompanies the materialisation of the Doctor's TARDIS.

W

WALLPAPER: Suddenly, redecorating the bedroom was something to look forward to. All you had to do was spend an unfeasibly large amount of money on a few rolls of *Doctor Who* wallpaper, featuring Peter Davison's likeness (and some Daleks and Cybermen). Short of getting in builders to turn your boudoir into a mock-up of the TARDIS console room, this was the best way to ensure that your favourite programme would permeate your dreams. However, it was also another example of merchandise that lost its value over time. Your rare acquisition is worth little when it's torn and dirty and only hanging on by virtue of the adhesive properties of its fungal growths. Those who had the foresight to keep a few rolls to one side can now reap the rewards on the open market; for those who slapped up the lot, the only sensible course is to call in the builders after all, to remove the whole wall and take it to a bank vault for safe-keeping. By a remarkable coincidence, we happen to know someone within whose bedchamber this historic *c.* 1983 wallcovering remains extant. It is indeed fortunate for this particular person that we are not above accepting bribes, or we'd have no alternative but to reveal his identity here. Wouldn't we Paul?

TEN SAD ITEMS OF MERCHANDISE

1: *Doctor Who* Tiles. Once your bedroom is taken care of, why not get grouting and transform the bathroom and kitchen into shrines to the Doctor too, with the application of these colourful items featuring artwork reditions of the fourth Doctor and some Daleks – funnily enough, exactly the same artwork that appears on the *Doctor Who* under-pants (see UNDERPANTS, *DOCTOR WHO*). Oh, and while you're at it don't forget that no fan's room is com-plete without a *Doctor Who* lampshade.

2: Dalek Baseball Cap. A rather limp eyestalk attachment made doubly certain that its wearers looked like dickheads.

3: Tom Baker Playsuit. Okay, we'll come clean: we're only slagging this one off because we can't get it in Large.

4: Bonnie Langford Figure. Did Dapol really believe that one Mel figure wasn't enough for fans' collections? Obviously they did, since a blue-clad version quickly joined the pink original; perhaps it was only poor sales that have since spared us from the inevitable red, yellow and green follow-ups that would have comprised a Bonnie Langford Power Rangers rip-off set. We wonder, too, if there's any truth in the rumour that leftover Mels were sold to the army for use as firing-range targets. One more thought: if the Dapol Cyberman and Mel figure are both made to the same scale, then Bonnie Langford must be 6'9" with a 58" chest.

5: Mothercare *Doctor Who* Slippers. Let's get this straight: purchased for small children with the sole (Hey, a pun! Well, nearly) intention of their being worn is fine. It's only when they are exhibited in a glass display case and gazed at in admiration that things get tragic. There were also some Dalek slippers-cum-booties in the sixties, but as they're now worth £200 they can't really be considered sad (though the pathetic individuals who'd spend £200 on them can).

6: *Doctor Who* Phonecards. Apparently these things lose their collectible value if they're used to make phone calls with. So what the bloody hell's the point of them?

7: *Doctor Who* Playmat. Only the sixth Doctor and Peri version, of course: the fourth Doctor and Leela one produced at the same time by the same firm is a must for any collection.

8: TARDIS Console Postcard. Not so much sad as misguided. We could be wrong, though: maybe the console did receive fan letters requesting signed photos.

9: *Doctor Who* Chess Set. Spending £600 or so on this is pretty sad, but you can just about get away with it by claiming: 'I've always wanted a really nice chess set, and what with me being a long-time *Doctor Who* fan and all, this one seemed appropriate.' Long-time fan or not, if you've sent off for the hundred or so supplemental monsters, companions, etc, there's really no hope.

10: The New Adventures. No, obviously we're larking about. Aren't they marvellous?

***

'WAR GAMES, THE': A fitting finale to the era of the second Doctor. This monsterless adventure managed to sustain its break-neck pace and edge-of-seat excitement throughout the course of ten whole episodes without becoming in the slightest bit boring (for the benefit of our American readership, this is what's called 'irony').

WELLS, H G: English novelist whose output included all-time classics of the science-fiction genre such as *The Shape of Things to Come, The War of the Worlds* and *The Time Machine*. His decision to write the latter in the first person has resulted in several film and TV productions (such as *Time After Time* and *The New Adventures of Superman*) featuring Wells himself as the inventor and pilot of the time-travelling device. A dramatised appearance in 'Timelash', however, was less than flattering. Here, the young Herbert George is inspired to write by the sight of the TARDIS and the myriad wonders of Karfel (though if ever a planet looked cheap enough to put anyone off writing SF . . .), insultingly suggesting that he didn't possess the imagination to concoct his own novel. The Doctor was seen enjoying

193

The Time Machine in 'The US Telemovie with the Pertwee Logo'. If we didn't know better, we'd suspect he was looking forward to angling for a share of the royalties. Or perhaps he was just marvelling at how much Wells had had to re-write his experiences to get a decent adventure yarn out of them.

WHITE CIRCLE, LARGE: Major component of a piece of artwork on page 67 of *The Doctor Who Annual 1977*. The editors presumably mistook it for a post-modernistic statement by artist Paul Crompton, and not, as was in fact the case, a desperate attempt to hide an abortive drawing. While we're at it, look up page 52 of the 1980 book and tell us what you think is going on there.

WHITEHOUSE, MARY: Founder of the National Viewers and Listeners Association, and guardian of the UK's morals. In these iniquitous times, it's all too easy to mock the heartfelt beliefs of such a well-meaning, compassionate lady ... so easy, in fact, that we can't resist it. After all, this daft old bat* has constantly pilloried *Doctor Who*, and even managed to get questions asked in Parliament about the end of 'The Deadly Assassin' part three. She felt that impressionable schoolchildren might re-enact the drowning sequence and accompanying freeze-frame, and the BBC were forced to edit their master copy accordingly. Now, we were both at school at that time, but our recollection of *Who*-themed playground games was that they consisted of: 'I'm a Dalek, I've extermi-nated you'; 'No you haven't, you missed'; 'Did not'; 'Did, did'; etc. Not one of our fellow students ever tried

* *Just our little joke, honest; we don't want to get the book pulped or anything.*

194

to hold a little chum's head underwater for a week. Undeterred, however, Mrs W continued her criticism of, amongst other stories, 'Vengeance on Varos', which proved that she had missed the whole point. Still, we have one thing to be grateful to the NVLA for: an attack from them has always proved to be the best tonic ratings could hope for.

WHITE ROBOTS: Colour photos from 'The Mind Robber' have revealed that these automata were nothing of the kind; they were in fact yellow in hue. Why lie about a thing like that?

WHIZZKID: Gian Sammarco's character in 'The Greatest Show in the Galaxy', which was written as a parody of anoraked fans. 'Although I never got to see it in the early days,' says Whizzkid of the Psychic Circus, 'I know it's not as good as it used to be.' Funny thing is, he was right. The circus, after all, had fallen into the hands of malign entities that caused it to become stagnant, employed unsuitable acts, refused to let it go and eventually caused its destruction.

WHO, DAVE: A *Doctor Who Magazine*'s typesetter's idea of a brilliant joke. Obviously, it wasn't – 'Dave Who'? Please. Look mate, if you're after getting the boot, at least try to go out in style.

WHO'D BE A *WHO* GIRL/BOY?: Being whisked off by the Doctor, if you'll pardon the expression, is the wish-dream of many *Who* fans. But why? Running up and down corridors, trying to keep all your hair on and your Badge for Mathematical Excellence intact, while various nasty monsters try to exterminate you, hardly sounds like fun. We don't suppose time travel is all it's cracked up to be either. Imagine visiting the scene of one of history's so-called great spectacles, the Charge of the Light Brigade for instance, only to discover that Hollywood did it better, albeit with the Union Jack upside down. Or meeting the creative genius who's been the source of so much inspiration throughout your life, only to find he's a bigger creep than the bloke who tried to feel you up in the pub last Friday night. It's just not worth having your illusions shattered for, is it?

WHODUNNIT: Misleadingly titled murder-mystery game show starring Jon Pertwee. Who never dunnit, he was the presenter.

WHOMOBILE: Kind of pseudo-futuristic Robin Reliant.

WHO 7: Don't you think it was a bit of a coincidence that Bessie's registration number switched from **WHO 1** to **WHO 7** just because the seventh Doctor turned up for a spin in her in 'Battlefield'? Are we supposed to believe it regenerated? If so, then surely it should have been **WHO 3** when Jon Pertwee drove it and **WHO 4** when Tom took the wheel. More likely it was a spot of self-indulgence from the production team, trying to be clever but failing totally. And after they'd gone to all that trouble with the UNIT passes, too.

WHOVIANS: A term coined by American *Doctor Who* fans to describe themselves and fellow American *Doctor Who* fans. Unfortunately, the appellation is becoming increasingly applied in this country, even though we've got by for decades as simply 'fans of the programme'. Trouble is, if we complain about the Whovian tag, we end up looking like those self-styled Trekkers who object to being labelled Trekkies. Like being called a Trekker is going to affect the way people perceive you: 'Hmm, a Trekker eh? You must be pedantic and sad, instead of merely sad like those pathetic Trekkies.'

TEN OTHER CRAP LABELS THAT COULD COLLECTIVELY BE APPLIED TO 'FANS OF THE PROGRAMME'

1: Doccers.
2: Doctorates.
3: Doctrines.
4: Doc-Heads.
5: Whooters.
6: Whomans.
7: Whoovers.
8: Whores.
9: Whookers.
10: Anorak-clad Wankers (Copyright *Loaded* 1996).

WOODEN ACTING: Having been transformed into a tree by the despicable Rani, Luke Ward was able to swing one branch like an arm, to prevent Peri from blundering into similar peril. We just thought we'd remind you of that scene; it brings a smile to our faces too.

WORLD WAR III: If the Doctor persists in averting this conflict how will we ever manage to get to World War VI by the 51st century?

WORKING TITLES: Confusing term for *Doctor Who* story titles that don't really work at all and thus are changed before transmission. 'The Claws of Axos', for instance, was known as 'Vampire from Space' until rather late in the day; in fact opening credits bearing that name were produced and it even got a mention in *Radio*

Times. This must have really annoyed the people who make the opening titles, if not those who publish *Radio Times*. It's possible to speculate on why some of these so-called working titles didn't make it: 'The Androids of Zenda' might have switched to Tara so that it wouldn't be quite so obvious which of Anthony Hope's Ruritanian adventures had been lifted to provide the plot; although if that's the case they might as well have stayed put. 'The War Game' could have become 'The Awakening' to prevent it being mistaken for an abridged version of Patrick Troughton's final outing. We shouldn't be surprised if 'The Return' was changed to 'Resurrection of the Daleks' so that some viewers might actually become interested enough to watch it. However, why then did 'Storm over Avallion' become 'Battlefield'? Unless it was felt that the former title made it sound a lot more enthralling than it actually was. Occasionally, dropping the working title causes problems later on: if only 'Terror of the Zygons' had stuck with one of its Loch Ness-based denominations we could have avoided the whole Skarasen/Borad debate.

TEN WORKING TITLES THAT MAKE YOU WONDER WHY THEY BOTHERED

1: 'The Space Wheel'.
2: 'The Sea Silurians'.
3: 'The Curse of Mandragora'.
4: 'The Dangerous Assassin'.
5: 'The Monster of Fang Rock'.
6: 'The Ribos File'.
7: 'Nightmare of Evil'.
8: 'Return of the Cybermen'.
9: 'Return of the Cybermen'.
10: 'Return of the Cybermen'.

X

XERONS: Inhabitants of the planet Xeros.

XEROS: Planet inhabited by Xerons.

'X-RANI AND THE UGLY MUTANTS': Story from the *Doctor Who Annual 1980*, mentioned here only because the 'X' section would have looked a bit pathetic otherwise.

Y

YARTEK, LEADER OF THE ALIEN VOORD: Speech-impaired rubber fetishist who tried to menace the Doctor on Marinus but was foiled when he tripped over his own flippers.

YARVELLING: Alien chronicles, discovered three decades ago by Earthman Terry Nation, revealed the existence of a race of metal-encased monsters created by this Skarosian scientist. However, a sceptic by the name of Davros is apparently contesting the authenticity of Nation's finds.

YETI ON THE TOILET IN TOOTING BEC: Jon Pertwee was always fond of suggesting that this would be a really scary thing indeed, thus justifying the fact that, instead of travelling to different planets, his Doctor stayed on Earth and fought off an unfeasible number of invasions. However, the statement has several logical flaws. The capacity of the Yeti to frighten anybody is arguable, even following director Douglas Camfield's decision to transform them from cuddly big teddy bears into cuddly big teddy bears with terrifying red fuzzy-felt eyes for 'The Web of Fear'. It also has to be said that it would be difficult for a Yeti to enter any public toilets in Tooting Bec without demolishing a turnstile entrance and leaving an obvious clue to its presence.

Even if you were to risk spending a penny despite this, it would be the Yeti itself that had most reason to fear, having been caught offguard in a compromising position. You would have plenty of time to escape while it was struggling to wipe its fur clean, washing its hands, etc. This claim is therefore a ridiculous one that fails to stand up to any sort of objective scrutiny.

'YOU'RE GETTING OLD, DOCTOR, YOUR WILL IS WEAK!': Line spoken in 'The King's Demons', open to misinterpretation.

YRCANOS: Last in a long line of alien letches wanting to get into Peri's leotard (not that there was much room in there). If the climax of 'Mindwarp' is not to be believed – and like the rest of it, we see no reason why it should be – and Peri did get hitched to the noisy monarch, it is unlikely that she did so because she liked the idea of becoming Queen of Krontep. She probably believed a wedding ring would deter the constant stream of galactic gropers.

Z

ZARBI: If ever there was such a thing as a pantomime ant, the costume designer need look no further than 'The Web Planet' for inspiration.

Z-CARS: In its time, a hugely popular week-night drama serial. The *Doctor Who* production team wanted to cash in on its popularity by having characters from the show make cameo appearances in 'The Feast of Steven', the Christmas '65 episode of 'The Daleks' Master Plan'. However, the offer to appear was declined by the *Z-Cars* team, who no doubt felt that getting up to pantomime-style antics in *Doctor Who* might affect the credibility and integrity of their programme. How things change.

ZEBADEE UNIVERSITY: Institute of Higher Education that John and Gillian Who attended after leaving their grandfather. We'd hate to speculate about how much learning goes on there, as presumably it's always time for bed.

TEN LANDMARK FIRSTS FROM THE PAGES OF *TV COMIC* (AND *COUNTDOWN* AND *TV ACTION*)

1: *TV Comic* issue 674. First there was Superman in

Action Comics issue 1. Then came Spider-Man in *Amazing Fantasy* issue 15. And, in 1964, another character destined to explode into the pages of his own magazine (though admittedly it took fifteen years for it to hit the newsstands) made his own comic strip debut: the one and only Dr Who.

2: *TV Comic* issue 694. 'On the Web Planet' was the first strip to get a proper title. *TV Comic's* policy of not bothering to name their early stories was contrary to the TV programme's practice of giving its early stories several titles. This unsatisfactory lack of denomination has since prompted researchers to think up their own names (come to think of it, this is the case with the TV series too). How thoughtful, if a bit sad. Oh yeah, 'On the Web Planet' was the first comic strip sequel to a television story (see if you can guess which one).

3: *TV Comic* issue 748. Featuring the debut of the Trods, this tale set out to dispel any notion that *TV Comic* needed (or, indeed, could afford) the Daleks; these robotic terrors were of their own devising and therefore free. They returned on several occasions, so the publishers certainly got their money's worth. However, it says a lot for *TV Comic's* loyalty to their creations that, when the rights to the Daleks were finally acquired (with issue 788), the Trods were the first to get the crap kicked out of them by Skaro's metal meanies.

4: *TV Comic* issue 872. What's this? John and Gillian being dumped in favour of Jamie? The appearance of another mechanical race from the series? Oh, it's all right: . . . although the Quarks in this tale look exactly like they did in 'The Dominators', the similarities end there. Phew, that's a relief. For one scary moment, we thought *TV Comic* was attempting to resemble its screen counterpart. Readers of the much-missed (by one or two of us) *Doctor Who – Classic Comics* will be aware that Mervyn Haisman and Henry Lincoln were less than happy to see their cuboid creations unexpectedly turn up in the strip, and attempted to prevent further illustrated Quark escapades. BBC Enterprises had to reassure the comic's publishers that they were safe to continue. But they did advise against going ahead with a plan to use the Yeti in a forthcoming story . . .

5: *TV Comic* issue 881. The debut of the Yeti in a *Doctor Who* comic strip. Well actually, it wasn't. For reasons outlined above, the Doctor's hairy adversaries were rechristened Ice Apes and underwent a drastic change of appearance. And all the more fearsome they were for it.

6: *TV Comic* issue 934. An absolutely amazing *TV Comic* first: a story that displays both imagination and respect for TV continuity. On television, the Time Lords had sentenced the Doctor to exile on Earth with a change of appearance thrown in. To bridge the gap between 'The War Games' and 'Spearhead from Space', the *TV Comic* editors devised a scenario in which the second Doctor was indeed exiled but somehow evaded the appearance-altering bit. The really good part happens at the end of the second Doctor's strip tenure. He is pursued to Earth by agents of the Time Lords (inconspicuously disguised as scarecrows), and as the Worzel Gummidge wannabes carry him back to the TARDIS he is even seen to regenerate (well, artist John Canning drew a wavy line around him, which is more than you got on the telly). Troughton's Doctor had another crack at eluding the Time Lords later: towards the end of the strip's run in *TV Comic*, he donned a long scarf, grew some curly hair and pretended to be Tom Baker.

7: *TV Comic* issue 944. The first appearance of Margaret Rutherford as the Doctor. Oh sorry, no, it's meant to be Jon Pertwee. The publishers must have won the pools or something, as they forked out to include both the Brigadier and Liz Shaw (although maybe they saved some cash by not bothering to pay for Pertwee's likeness).

8: *Countdown* issue 1. The first time *Doctor Who* appeared in a good comic. The glossy photogravure *Countdown* lasted for around a year before regenerating into the matt-finish *TV Action*. This incarnation lasted slightly longer than its predecessor, before succumbing to the dreaded comic-book malaise of amalgamation. For *Doctor Who*, this meant a return to the familiar pages of *TV Comic*, alongside old friends like 'Mighty Moth' and 'The TV Terrors'. Ah well, it was nice while it lasted; so what if the third Doctor sometimes drove a car called Betsy and we were treated to yet another solution to the mystery of the *Marie Celeste*?

9: *TV Comic Annual 1976*, 'Wotan's Warriors'. A story unremarkable but for the fact that it was drawn by John M Burns, a veritable god amongst British comic illustrators. He's drawn everyone who matters from Dan Dare to Judge Dredd – even Jane of the *Daily Mirror*. His telefantasy output includes *UFO*, *The Tomorrow People* and *Space: 1999*. Naturally, he was the obvious choice to handle the artwork for Colin Baker's sixth Doctor graphic novel *Age of Chaos*, and he did start the project. Perhaps we'll never know the full story but it's our guess that he felt the whole thing was beneath his significant talent and left it for someone else to finish. Colin Baker shouldn't take it personally, however: at the time of writing, James Bond fans are still waiting for John to draw issue 3 of *A Silent Armageddon*, issue 2 of which came out several years ago.

10: *TV Comic Annual 1979*. The Doctor's companion, the bespectacled Miss Young, appears without introduction in 'The Sea Devil' (no relation). She's pretty tough and comes out with stuff like: 'Let us hurry Doctor, if the evil thing should return . . .'; 'It comes . . .'; and 'Back, sea devil', whilst attacking the poor seaweed creature with her trusty knife. You don't suppose it could have been Leela wearing a clever Clark Kent-inspired disguise do you? Nah, couldn't be.

ZERONS: Race of aliens from the *TV Action* third-Doctor comic strip 'The Enemy from Nowhere', not to be confused in any way, shape or form with the completely different and entirely dissimilar race of aliens who appeared in the *TV Action* third-Doctor comic strip 'Zeron Invasion' a few weeks later (nor with the Xerons off the telly).

ZOG: Hairy alien companion from *The Ultimate*

Adventure, who later turned against the Doctor and was last seen glaring malevolently at him from the window of the Queen Victoria pub.

———————◆———————

TEN(ISH) OTHER COMPANIONS WHO AREN'T OFF THE TELLY, OR FROM THE NEW/MISSING ADVENTURES EITHER, FOR THAT MATTER

1: Louise. Yet another member of the Who family.

2: Jason. What an overwhelming sense of relief we felt when Graham Smith was cast as this *Ultimate Adventure* character and not, as rumoured, Jason Donovan.

3: Crystal. Babe!

4: Jenny. Perhaps there is some logic in casting an actress who's already played one companion on television as a different companion in a stageplay when the actor who is playing the Doctor hasn't already played the Doctor on television. The producers obviously thought so as they didn't want Jon Pertwee, but cast Wendy Padbury to appeal to the fans. Yeah, actually we can see it now.

5: Jimmy. Perhaps we shouldn't have included this other *Seven Keys* character when we know sod all about him. Apart from his being played by someone called James Matthews of course, although we know sod all about him too. Mind you, *The Seventies* book reckons (and we believe everything it says, of course we do) that Simon Jones stood in on a couple of occasions. So who got lumbered with the stilts, then?

6: John and Gillian. Introduced in Dr Who's debut *TV Comic* strip because the publishers were initially too cheap to fork out on proper companions. The funny thing about the Who kids was that they started out as young children and matured into teenagers. This natural ageing process is virtually unknown in the world inhabited by comic-book characters, even in strips that purport to take a realistic approach, let alone in *TV Comic*, a publication that you could hardly accuse of having pretentions in that direction. This is why Popeye was never done for GBH and the crew of *Fireball XL5* never died when they space-walked without spacesuits on.

7: Frobisher. It's hardly practical for a shape-shifter to go around in the form of a penguin is it? They're not the fastest, most proficient all-terrain-covering species in the universe. Presumably he was just easier to draw that way, or maybe someone at Marvel liked him. No one else did. Other equally exciting Marvel companions included Sharon, Gus and Olla. How memorable they all were.

8: Jeremy. Git!

9: Cora. We hadn't intended to include companions who didn't get beyond script stage, but this early-film-draft 'Time Lady' was to have been played by Caroline Munro and we just like thinking about her really. Especially that bit in *The Golden Voyage of Sinbad* when she's lifted out of the boat and . . .

10: George. What do you mean, 'Who?' Surely you remember good old George Mortimer from *Doctor Who and the Invasion from Space* (a slim annual-format Hartnell 'Missing Adventure' from 1966). Why, he even brought his wife Helen and the two kids, Ida and Alan, along for the ride to Andromeda. This proved to be advantageous, because Ida saved the universe by having a tantrum and throwing her jelly bowl at something important.

ZORG AND ORG: Dalek proprietors of the Inter-Gallactic (sic) Record Shop on Gamma-Ursa 9 on the icy edge of the galaxy. The Doctor barely avoided extermination, or even obliteration, when he popped in to pick up a copy of the 'Genesis of the Daleks' LP from the Alien Menace section. It was perhaps unwise of him, then, to go back for the *Doctor Who* theme tune a year later. Its repeated use aside, this half-page advertising strip was remarkable for eschewing the traditional 'Vworp' TARDIS sound in favour of a more innovative 'Thooooooommm'.

BIBLIOGRAPHY

Every publication written about *Doctor Who* since the year dot, of course, but especially *that* page in the *Doctor Who – Companions* book (not the one by JN-T).

INDEX